THE INFORMANT
A CONTEMPORARY PARABLE

The Informant
A Contemporary Parable

John Adamson

DEBTS OF GRATITUDE

The above are due to many people whose support and encouragement have been vital throughout the process of committing this story to paper. I am fortunate that the outcome has been influenced so much by those I am lucky to call friends.

I was equally fortunate to have a chat with Stuart and the talented Townend family some time ago in Keswick about the public response to the song 'Vagabonds', the lyrics of which provided the inspiration for 'The Informant'. I am therefore immensely grateful to them for this and all their songs which play such a prominent global role in Christian worship today.

Hilary Skinner has meticulously read every word so many times that there are sections of the work which she can remember by heart. Her thoughtful criticism, encouragement and legendary patience over many months have been inspirational to me. Peter Lupson spent hours with me on detailed aspects of the manuscript, sharing invaluable wisdom and sensitivity. Rev. Al Metcalfe and his colleague, Rev. Dr. Al Rodgers, generously offered guidance, advice and thoughtful appreciation at key moments in the crafting of the story. My team of draft readers Jane and Laurence Bozier, Roger Hind, Kevin Marley and David Jack have played important roles with their feedback and attention to detail.

Writing about anyone's Christian journey, factual or fictional, leads inevitably to reflecting on one's own. The seed of the gospel was planted in my heart by four patient Welsh friends at the time, one Sandra, two Siâns, and an Eirwyn. I know now what a frustration and annoyance I must have been in response. Unknown to them and nearly 20 years later, that seed germinated through the kindness of the late Rev. Ivan Burke, who was a wonderful and remarkable Catholic priest, my wife Caroline, Rev. Steve James and his wife Rachel, and later the inspirational witness of Hugh Bradby, Christian colleagues and students at Kingsmead School, Rev. Philip Venables, Rev. David Vestergaard and his inimitable wife Ash, as the truth of the gospel transformed me. The annual Keswick Convention too has been a source of clear teaching and uplifting worship.

Finally, but no less importantly, Caroline and my daughter Rachel have also graciously given me the time I needed to work on the story, without complaint. Words cannot express my huge personal gratitude for their encouragement and love especially over such an intensive period of writing.

And to those whom I may have inadvertently omitted, I also offer my heartfelt thanks!

John Adamson

PROLOGUE

THE INFORMANT
A CONTEMPORARY PARABLE?

How can a story from our own time and culture be a parable? To understand this, it is helpful to look briefly at what exactly constitutes a parable.

'Paraballo' is a Greek verb which can be translated as the act of placing one thing alongside another so that the two can be compared.

Parables were a commonly used teaching technique from the oral tradition. They were short stories, usually but not always fictitious, which invited the listener to learn something about themselves by analogy with the characters or events in the plot.

Parables evolved into a written form as technology and culture changed. Shakespeare, in plays such as Julius Caesar, used historical factual events to ask his audience to challenge perceptions about the time in which they lived, using the voices of the theatrical tradition to retain the power of the oral tradition. In the modern day, video clips can serve the same purpose, where actors' voices are heard performing from the author's script.

Jesus used parables powerfully in the gospels to audiences who were listening carefully to his words as he spoke to them. In the story of the Prodigal Son and others, we are encouraged to see how we are like one or more of the characters.

'The Informant' is humbly offered as a contemporary parable which lays a fictitious story of real-life issues and events alongside your life and mine, inviting us to engage with the characters we meet as they speak of their experiences, hopes, fears and failings. Perhaps we can be drawn into this story, then, to discern a relevance to life as we live it today.

The 2011 song 'Vagabonds' reminded me vividly of all those invited to eat at God's table. Before reading the story, it may be helpful to listen to or read the lyrics of this Bible-based work.

CHAPTER 1

The French postman grinned as he placed a single envelope into Judy's outstretched fingers and thumb. He bowed playfully, a twinkle in his eye. At the lowest point of his gesture, he spoke softly and respectfully, "Madame."

Madame smiled back and thanked him. "Merci Monsieur." She hid her impulsive grin as he twisted round towards the door after executing a textbook Gallic shrug.

Madame glanced at the handwritten address below the stamp and closed the communal entrance door to the flats on the concreted scene she wished she loved. The high-rise windows of her working-class Parisian estate glinted in the outer suburban summer morning sun. For Judy Elderman and her husband, this was not a great place to live. They were still going to miss it when their time was up.

"Roger?"

The Rev. Herbert Roger Elderman didn't look up

from his book. "What is it?" Her husband's voice revealed a lack of enthusiasm to engage with his wife at that point.

"Looks like another letter from that man. Called you Herbert. The chap who you said thinks God wants us to move back to England. Shall I open it?"

Roger's tone showed that his enthusiasm remained constant. "He's called Jonah. Let's do it after lunch. We've got Yvon and Jeanne coming over to discuss developing the music group. I'm not sure I want to face up to anything else right now. Maybe we should serve a glass of sauvignon with the starter?"

"There's a bottle of champagne in the fridge. But just be careful with Yvon. We had enough trouble with several of your English friends thinking he was a girl. They didn't realise there was a boy's version of his name as well as a girl's. And he's only just getting over what happened last time, after you'd seen this Jonah chap's first letter."

Roger raised his eyebrows. "Remind me?"

"Yes, dear. You were a bit overwrought, as I recall. I asked you what the matter was. You told me you were finding it hard to stop spending every moment working."

"Was that the time you told me to relax and read a bit more? Find something light, I think you said."

"That's right. I'm not sure if you did, though."

"Judy, would I ever not follow your words of wisdom?"

"Well, I asked you the title of the book you had

chosen, and you informed me you had found something really light. A book on anti-gravity."

Roger glanced at his wife and grinned. "Ah yes. Great book. Light? It was impossible to put down. Now, seriously, what actually happened with Yvon?"

"You didn't make allowances for the fact that he is still learning English. You asked him if he would like to start lunch off with grace."

"Ah, yes. I remember. He said he'd rather sit by Jeanne. It was a bit embarrassing. He was confused. I had to give thanks myself."

"That was it, yes."

"No wonder he requested to sit between Jeanne and me today."

Judy smirked "Ah. Yes. It was not an experience he would wish to repeat, even though we explained later what grace means when you share a meal. By the way, I've decided that, once grace has been said, we'll serve a nice pâté for starters today."

Roger laughed. "Brussels pâté is most appropriate for the pair of them."

Some years earlier, the Eldermen, as they were known by their less imaginative home counties friends, had taken the opportunity to give up their ministry in a suburban Surrey church to move to the French capital in a missionary role. And here they were, accustomed and in service to their adopted and diverse, if small, flock.

Belgian national Jeanne and her African husband Yvon had been sent to join their number a year ago.

Jeanne was a life-long Christian from a Christian family, and Yvon had become a Christian after meeting her. He had been born to Congolese parents in Kinshasa, staying on in Belgium after studying in Brussels.

Now the pair of them were finishing their final training placement with Roger and Judy for a missionary role. Jeanne was bilingual courtesy of her English mother, and both she and her husband were accomplished musicians. Yvon's English was almost fluent although he was hesitant at times, but he was proving a fast learner who was growing quickly in confidence. And now, they were all friends.

Judy and Roger had met soon after university. Judy, abused mentally and physically as a child by her father, had instantly fallen for the handsome young minister whose love and steady calmness she craved. Her case had never been resolved despite intensive police investigation. From the most difficult of starts in life, she had come to share his faith which had given her a powerful ongoing source of strength in the rebuilding of her life.

From those early days, Judy's problems with low self-esteem and depression, a condition common to many who, like her, had suffered a similar dreadful early life experience, continued to surface. Roger had remained serene and supportive, seeing through the bluff of her self-deprecating humour.

Encouraging the development of that, but at his own expense, had been his positive response, and over the intervening years their marriage was blessed, usually, with the therapeutic ability to share dry wit. There was also a growing sense of a call to respond by supporting the disadvantaged and the desperate, which had ultimately led them to French soil. Here, they had dedicated themselves to living amongst the forgotten, the rejected, the stateless and the marginalised, offering a real hope to those open to receiving it.

But Judy's issues, suffered as a child, never went away completely, were sometimes too close at hand and rarely out of reach. Roger prayed frequently for Judy's complete healing.

Humour, dry or not, was not featuring today in this part of the conversation. "I'm not going." Roger pushed a coffee mug to one side. "There's still so much to be done here. I'm not going."

Judy stared. "I'm right with you on that. The people who have come to believe, those who haven't but will, the refugees who've arrived, there's work to be finished. And I don't want to go home."

She pushed the unopened envelope into the space where his mug had been. "I wish you had never opened that first letter. Not that you bothered to show me it. None of this would have started. Anyway, why does he use your full name? Look, Herbert Roger Elderman. Doesn't that just irritate you? Not even a Reverend as a title."

"You know what, I'm not even going to open it." Roger was calm. "Not for a day or two, anyway. In fact,

I'm going to put it out of sight. Out of sight, out of mind."

"Just because your Reverend title was missing on the envelope?" Judy quipped. The humour was back, but Roger missed it.

"Come on, you know me better than that. I don't do status. You can't help people, serve their needs and so on, if they have to call you something that is a barrier. It makes me sound holier than others. I can't face opening the letter yet, that's all. I've got work to do for Sunday, some people to visit, and I can't think beyond that. Ok? Let's get on with life – and more importantly, lunch!"

CHAPTER 2

"That was good fun." Judy smiled. Lunch had, like their guests, gone down well.

"They're a talented pair. Real missionary leadership material. I'm so pleased that Jeanne is working on translating some worship songs from English, and Yvon is writing one of his own in French. Could be the start of something big. I played that 'Vagabonds' song to them a couple of days ago, and they were both really taken with it." Roger was enthused. "The song speaks directly into their situation – and ours. Yvon's been looking up some of the English terms in the song. He's certainly learned about different types of sin there as well as having some unexpected vocabulary to deal with!"

Judy continued to smile. "But Yvon seemed fascinated with Liverpool. Of all things. That was a bit odd, all those questions, seeing as neither of us know the place. I know Jeanne's got an old friend she told me about – I remember she moved there from Wales – but that's all. Liverpool's not known for its vagabonds, is it?"

"I'm sure it has had its fair share."

Judy needed reassurance. "It's a decent place, though, isn't it?"

"Depends whom you ask."

"How safe is it?"

Roger paused a moment. "Well, some of the place is still a bit like here, you know, where even the pit bull terriers go around in pairs."

"Have they improved the place?"

Roger smirked. "There are areas that now even have trees. I jest, but a few decades ago, it suffered major decline, and now it's changed. They even do cruise ships now. Anyway, most people of his age have heard about the Beatles and know some of their songs. Or maybe Jeanne's been talking about her old friend who lives there. It's hard to know." Roger was less than convincing.

"Been studying it, have you? Why didn't you tell Yvon all this at lunchtime? You were very quiet." Judy's forehead wrinkled.

"I'm just a bit preoccupied with something, that's all. But Yvon's writing his worship song, and that's so important, more than Jeanne's translations. We want our worship to be in the culture of the country we're in."

Judy was pensive. "Ok, but there's a hub of major British worship songwriters based on the south coast, you know, down Brighton way, including the man who wrote Vagabonds. I don't know of any from Liverpool. What's more, I'm not sure exactly how much worship music was written by the Beatles either." Her expression creased slightly, then turned into a smile.

Roger couldn't help doing likewise. "Anyway, it's up north. You wouldn't like it. Now then, we both have plenty to do, so let's get on, shall we? Pastoral plans to update."

Judy reverted to French. "Allons-y. Revenons à nos moutons." Her face broke into a grin as it was Roger's turn to look pensive.

Pensiveness didn't last long. "Yer waaa?" he retorted, attempting a scouse accent. Roger's knowledge of common French sayings was limited to hardly any. "What is that about? Doesn't 'mouton' mean sheep?"

Judy pressed home the point. "It's an expression which means 'let's get back to business'. But yes, it refers to a shepherd wasting time talking when he should be looking after his flock. Like you, dear."

Roger nodded sagely. "Shall we get on?"

CHAPTER 3

Almost 400 miles away, the chatter around the gentle pastel uniformity of a John Lewis café in the heart of the city evidenced the presence of international visitors, local people and tourists from around the UK. Roger was quite right; Liverpool had indeed bounced back from decline. And it was humming. Absolutely humming. Two men, who were clearly not humming, sat down at a corner table and looked sombrely at each other.

"What are we going to do?" The bright-eyed questioner was Pete, a well-dressed retiree whose international professional career had accustomed him to leadership, especially in crisis management. Despite the optimism in Pete's eyes, he wore the expression of a man with a crisis to be managed.

"Where do you want me to start?" Harry looked at him whimsically. He was the older of the pair, by a good fifteen years. A former science teacher, he had an analytical mind. The two men shared a mutual respect.

Pete laid out the agenda. "Do we give up? Do we get everyone to agree to join a church? There might be something suitable out there. Do we go back to meeting again in Martha's front room? Do we close up and put it all down as passing a sell-by date? There's not as many of us as there were, and one fewer since Dilys passed away. We will miss Dilys, but more than that we will miss her drive, her energy, her input. And don't forget that the police visit we had over historic child abuse allegations didn't exactly put us in a good light locally, even though we didn't exist as a group when it was supposed to have happened. It's not a great time to be trying to expand, is it?"

"Tricky to say the least." Harry acquiesced.

Pete nodded slowly. "Tough, Harry, it is tough. I do recall Dilys saying that we are not just dealing with the relevance of the gospel to modern life and its power to change people for the better. She said there was now even a feeling that the gospel, and therefore Christianity, contains something poisonous, you know, toxic. The world we live in today has ideas which sometimes fly in the face of the values Dilys had."

Harry agreed. "Pete what we need to do is to identify exactly what we are about, you know, our essence, our fundamental reason for what we are doing."

"Spot on, my friend."

Harry paused to stir his coffee in a deliberate manner. "Ok. Let's go back to the start, shall we? Where did our journey begin?"

Pete gave Harry a you-know-as-well-as-I-do glance but decided to humour him. "As you will recall, my friend, it was those evening classes we'd signed up for on 'Philosophy for Beginners'. You and I went along."

"Then what?" Harry was determined. "Tell me your own recollection of it, Pete."

Pete was doubting the value of telling his friend what they both knew but he took a deep breath and continued. "So we spent a couple of terms looking at all kinds of explanations of the meaning of life. One of the class was a lady called Dilys. I'd known her for some time. During discussion times, she spoke of God with a kind of authority. We made a point of chatting to her later. The three of us went for coffee. She asked us if we would like to talk some more, away from the class. We agreed. Then she said she had a friend, who worked in a local library, who might find a few more folk who were also curious. So we got together as a discussion group in the beginning, just meeting once a month. Why were we there? I guess we were all looking for meaning in our lives."

"Exactly." Harry was firm. "So Dilys's librarian friend Martha offered her home as a meeting point for the first few sessions. And very subtly, Dilys led us on a kind of journey of discovery. We enjoyed each other's company, grew a little and so we moved to meet on some Sunday mornings in a working-class suburban scout hut."

"Agreed, Harry. What seems most important to you now?"

"We must always remember how, where, and why we began, so we continue the same journey. Primarily, we are still a discussion group which welcomes new people. Some of us have moved further along the Christian journey than others, for sure, but it seems that the more you travel down the path, the more questions you have. I'd love to say I was a Christian, but I'm not there yet. I think you might be. So, do we get some sort of magic moment when we know? Do we feel something dramatic happen to us?"

There was a rhetorical element to Harry's questions, so Pete restricted himself to one remark before letting him continue. "We're all learning, Harry, all of us."

Harry did not hesitate. "In my view the scout hut works well. Many people won't go into a church building these days, because they are wary of what they'll find there. But a scout hut? No problem. So as a group, we threaten no-one, and we read the Bible together these days, discuss it, and learn from it in our own way, by discovering meaning, rather than being told it. Dilys was never a preacher to us, she was a guide."

"I'm not sure if it's appropriate for a guide to be found in a scout hut, Harry!"

Harry missed the humour. "No, Pete, it was Dilys who chose it. It was also Dilys who called it the chapel. She had a sense of irony, the old girl, and she was Welsh – you know, church or chapel. She had many misgivings about church so she was definitely chapel!"

Pete's look became serious. "Have we been badly

impacted by the child abuse issue? What are your thoughts on that, Harry?"

Harry looked nonplussed. After a moment, he looked down. "It's a serious one, Pete. The trouble is, when this issue is suspected, everyone has a duty to act. Investigations have to be undertaken. I don't know who pointed the police in our direction, but I suppose things could have been worse. At least no-one from our chapel was arrested, but people always make judgements. I think the damage was just that we got tarred with that particular brush."

Pete looked at him. "The more I find out, the more I realise how tough the culture we live in today can be for Christians. Dilys's views conflicted frequently with the way people do life today, especially in the West."

Harry agreed. His voice grew more confident. "You're right. It's the same everywhere, and the effect is more and more churches closing and being turned into luxury homes. Like the pubs. Depressing, really. Can we go against the flow? We're talking community here. And times are hard too. Austerity has hit everyone in these parts, especially around the city. Added to those child sexual abuse suspicions, there's this humanism thing, especially when it is aggressive, which has meant people are wary of any kind of religious group, and that seems to include our chapel. It's hard for new people to join us if their family, friends and neighbours are going to see them as some kind of freak."

"Harry, I don't disagree with you. Just going back a

step, Dilys was very aware of the way churches were being perceived, and she believed that there was a message which lay beneath it all which we had to uncover. She used an interesting phrase. She said it was a question of what she called God's outrageous grace and unconditional love."

"So what she was saying was that the message had more power than the mess man has made?"

"On every front, Harry. Power was the thing. Dilys said that since the time of Jesus, the message had had the power to defy every persecution and every attempt to restrict, control or obliterate it, and it had reached even more people as a result. They had felt its power, she said. It's the same with what's going on today. And remember, Dilys never seemed to be leading us, but after each session we seemed to understand more. We got stuff for ourselves, so there was a way open to believing it. She was one clever lady, that's for certain. We figure out the meaning of the Bible together. We find the answers to our own questions. Dilys was taking us forward on a journey, for sure, but it was our adventure."

"And that, Pete, is what must go on. We must keep moving forwards." Harry was determined. "I am sure you didn't bring me out here just to help you end our journey in some kind of nice way, Pete. Wind the project up? Close the chapel? Dilys would turn in her urn."

Pete sipped his cappuccino. "Yes, I agree. My thoughts are similar, have been every day. So no, I just wanted to sound you out. You're up for the fight. You've confirmed what I thought. Now, there's something I have to tell you."

Harry looked up.

"You're going to tell me old Dilys was something of a dark horse and left us a stash of cash, aren't you!" He pulled a sardonic face.

Pete opened his eyes wide. "She certainly was a dark horse. Who told you?"

Harry's face changed swiftly. "She did, Dilys told everyone she was going to do that. But no-one believed her. Me included. And I still don't. You're having me on, Pete. She lived in a terraced house near Anfield. Two up, two down, rented. She just went a bit vague about money in her later days. I bet you haven't seen any money yet, and personally, I don't think there is any." Harry hesitated. "Anyway, how much is it?"

"All I know, Harry, is that I've been called to her solicitor's office next Monday, and there is a pecuniary bequest. I am going to hope in the meantime that God will guide us to do what he wants, and that he will make the way ahead clear."

Harry nodded.

There was a dampness in the air when Monday finally arrived. Pete took a taxi into town and paid the driver off outside the solicitor's office. The secretary ushered him into the solicitor's presence and closed the door as they exchanged niceties.

"Essentially I have good news for you." The solicitor

straightened his tie. "Before I tell you about the bequest, there's a phrase with which she prefaces her legacy. This will perhaps mean more to you than it does to me, but her will quotes something that looks like a strapline in marketing speak, 'All One in Christ Jesus'."

Pete found that his index finger was wagging purposefully in the solicitor's direction. "Yes, Dilys used to go to a convention every year up in the Lake District. I've heard quite a bit about it. It's in Keswick. Dilys liked it because, like her, they didn't do denominations – Catholics, Congregationalists, Methodists, Anglicans, Baptists ...and all the rest. She had no time for that kind of thing, with all their superstructures. She just saw everyone as Christians. Or non-Christians."

The solicitor ignored the wagging finger and checked his notes. "Well, Dilys goes on to express a wish that the proceeds of her estate be used by you to, and I quote, 'rebuild our chapel'. She says 'our', but she's bequeathed everything she had to you. However, I have to say that there is no legal compulsion for you to follow her wishes. Dilys seems to have had every confidence in you, so effectively she has left the decision up to your own discretion."

Ten minutes later, the same driver turned up in response to Pete's call and they headed straight to Harry's address. Moments later, Harry was ebullient. "No more scout hut! We can get somewhere proper, with settees or sofas maybe, dignified, comfortable, warm, so we can have even better discussions, and really grow!"

Pete looked down. "Harry, think! I'm not sure that is what Dilys meant."

CHAPTER 4

In a café around the corner from the Arc de Triomphe, Roger was nervously drinking a Perrier water with Jeanne, who sat in front of an untouched decaffeinated coffee. It was Sunday afternoon, and Judy was out visiting a Syrian refugee family who had been recently housed close to the flat. Yvon was at home, working on his new song.

Roger's tone was confidential. "We've got to keep this secret. No-one else must know. It'll be the end of it if Judy finds out."

"I know." Jeanne looked serious. "But there will be a way. I'll get in touch when there's something definite. Just wait for me."

It was dark when he got back. Judy had been in a while.

"Your dinner's in the fridge. I'm having an early night. I can't be bothered with food tonight."

Roger finished the plate of food and after praying, retired tired. Judy was already asleep. But try though he would, thoughts were whirling around in his head and he couldn't settle. He knew the problems he would face in the morning. Her self-esteem would be flat. She would be listless and evasive. Evasive. He remembered his words to Jeanne.

Morning came. "Coffee, Mrs Elderman?" Roger affected cheeriness. Judy grunted and pointed to the bedside table.

Two sips later, she came to. "I dreamt last night."

"Was it awful?"

"No. Not like before. I just kept seeing a clock face. It was counting down. Like on a quiz show. It buzzed. Like a timer."

"Anything else? It rather sounds like you've been watching too much daytime tv."

"There was, actually. I dreamt about Yvon. It was bizarre. He was pointing to a huge bottle of champagne. He was showing me it. Then he was opening it. It was definitely Yvon. What's that all about?"

Roger's features betrayed a degree of relief. "God does use dreams, for sure. But not all the time. However, it does sound as if you might have something to celebrate soon. That's positive. Can't wait!" He looked at his bedside table. The letter he hadn't opened was still there. He carefully placed his coffee cup on it, covering the address. Judy watched him.

"When are you opening that?"

"How big was that bottle?" Roger's mind was on the dream.

"Bigger than a magnum."

"Ice cream or Champagne?" Roger lifted an eyebrow.

"The latter. Twice a magnum. Why?"

"That's a Jereboam. Biblical name."

"You'll be telling me it's definitely a dream message from God next. Now, what about the letter? When are you opening it?"

Roger grew serious. "I've told you, we are not going back to the UK. The letter? Not now, and probably not ever. Never." Roger's voice betrayed a strain. "I'm going to hide it if it bothers you that much. I'm going out for a walk to clear my head."

Five minutes later, Jeanne had agreed to meet him in the café on the corner.

Roger greeted her. "Judy's on to us, I'm sure. She must suspect we're up to something."

"She can't be. What have you told her?"

"Nothing. She's already unsettled. She dreamt last night. She knows I'm out of the flat more than I used to be before this all started. And we had a letter from someone telling us to go back to the UK."

"Yes. You told me you had had that."

"A second one came. The postman put it into her hand."

"What did it say?"

"I don't know. I haven't opened it yet."

"Are you going to?"

"No. Not yet. She's got enough to cope with. Jeanne, I'm scared about the future"

Jeanne looked concerned. "You? Scared?"

"I am. It's nagging at me. I simply can't give up and go back to the UK. We must complete what we started. The mission – and us. I'm not ready to throw in the towel."

"You can. If God is really calling you to do that, you have no choice."

"He can't be. We're doing his work here, and it's nowhere near finished. We've hardly started. And you and I, we have unfinished business, don't we?"

Jeanne looked at him. "Yes, if that's what you want to call it."

"She's struggling right now, Jeanne, the old issues. Flashbacks, I'm sure of it, vivid recollections, the fear, the horrible moments. Uncertainty over where we are and what we do is the last thing she needs. She needs routine."

"It's tough on you, Roger, so tough." She patted his arm affectionately. "But you know, I'm with you. And we are not giving up now. We've done the hard bit. It's time to do your part. We must go through with this and do what we need."

CHAPTER 5

There was nowhere quite like an authentic French café in Liverpool, but there was a city centre corner pub. Pete and Harry had convened a meeting there. They were alone.

Unconcerned by the attendance, Harry opened the meeting. "Pete, I believe that there's only three types of people in the world."

"Christians, Muslims and Hindus?" Pete ventured.

"No. People who can do maths and ones who can't,"

Pete nodded. "In that case we are quorate."

Harry reached for his coat playfully. "Does that mean I can go? I'm not sure I like being quorate. Is it painful?"

Pete winced. "No. Just walk gently. Yes, you can go. To the bar. You go there often enough when you're on your own, you'll be fine. Then we'll begin, even if there's just the two of us."

Two minutes later, Harry was back. "I'm sure it wasn't my round. Cheers anyway." He supped at his pint. "Nice beer this one. I popped out for a couple at lunchtime and it was ok, but this is much better. Cheers!"

Pete raised his sparkling mineral water in response and sipped it.

Harry pulled a face. "Never thought I'd see the day that, by the pint, a glass of water would cost more than beer."

Pete put his glass down. "You are quite keen on your beer, aren't you?"

"Dilys." Harry smiled before he looked at Pete. "Let's get down to brass tacks, my friend. What did she mean us to actually do about rebuilding the chapel?"

Pete looked at Harry. "What else do you remember of her? Dark horse, you said."

Harry stroked his cheek. "Dilys? Quite a bit. Definitely kept a lot to herself. I found out she lived in my neighbourhood after we met. I'm a southerner myself, and Dilys made me feel at home up here."

Pete recalled the moment. "Yes, I remember you moving up to the area. Dilys mentioned it. Happy days, Harry!"

Harry acknowledged the compliment. "I liked what Dilys said to us as a group. There was a peace about her which I'd never seen with anyone else. She kept it very simple. She spoke about God in straightforward terms and Pete, I thought, if it is for everyone, it has to be a simple message. But she seemed to have an authority to what she said, like she had been inspired by something.

Like a power of some kind that she was channelling." He stopped and looked at his friend.

Pete was already nodding. "She did. It was more than words, wasn't it?"

Harry found himself nodding too. "Yes, that lady had something, and I felt I wanted some of it. So, the whole thing hooked my interest, grabbed me, and encouraged me to look for whatever she had for myself. We developed a strong bond of friendship after that. Me and Dilys. Not God. Or maybe all three of us. If God exists, can he be your friend in that way?"

Pete said nothing.

Harry continued. "Dilys told me she had worked with that dentist in town for years, you know, as a dental nurse. She was still there when I met her. But she never forgot her skills when she retired. It was part of her, dental health. She even gave me a new toothbrush the week before she died. Insisted on taking the old one away. A true professional. Very thorough on the hygiene."

Harry paused for a mouthful of beer. "A dark horse to the last. Latterly she had me running mysterious errands for her, saying it was God's work I was helping with. I had a feeling that I could trust her that it was. Still got one left to do, if I'm honest. But if there is such a thing as a godly woman, Pete, she's one of them, especially as she'd known tragedy in her life."

Pete nodded thoughtfully. "Ok. I guess she told you that. Did that colour her beliefs? What was the Gospel according to Dilys?"

"Good question. You knew her as well as I did. Dilys read widely, yet she had no time for anything clever, or intellectual, but didn't suffer fools either. Like I say, she said that God's work was very simple, and that God will one day judge us all. She seemed to know that for certain. She claimed that God's verdict would be final. There wouldn't be a Court of Appeal. And it would be perfectly fair. Dilys believed that not one of us comes up to God's standards of perfection. She was definitely right in one thing: I know myself that we all have an in-built sense of justice in us and a sense of our own guilt."

Pete interrupted. "And she told you that those who accept Jesus and acknowledge their wrongdoing will be saved, yes?"

"That's right, Pete. Dilys read me the account of what happened at Calvary, where she explained what was going on. I'm still getting my head round all this, but she said that, well, we all get stuff wrong in life, and that's true. And she said we all feel guilty about the past too, and that's also true. She said about God judging us and that not one of us could stand before him with a clear conscience, because we'd all done wrong."

"Remember it's not just you." Pete was reassuring.

Harry was not to be stopped. "But she said that if we accepted that he was the son of God, and then we followed him, Jesus would take all that we do that is bad, then deal with it for us. Like we are in court, found guilty and someone steps in and tells you they'll do the punishment for you."

"How did that make you feel when she said that?"

"Baffled, to be honest. It was words, and I knew there was more than just words to Dilys. She had this power in her from somewhere, this incredible force which seemed sometimes to drive her life. But I read the Bible for myself to find out more."

"What did you find?"

Harry took a deep breath. "When I read it for myself, I did see how awful and horrific it was. He was abused and spat on. His dignity was taken away totally. If you want to know what political correctness looks like, do not start there. What that guy went through made the tough times I have had seem like a walk in the park. He was flogged mercilessly, an innocent man who seemed to have just loved all those he came across. He had this power to make people better, to calm the sea, to bring people back to life after they'd died. And so they killed him on a wooden cross. They drove big nails through his wrists and ankles to hold him up there. Horrific. Just horrific."

"Had Dilys told you what happened next?"

"I didn't believe it, Pete, this coming back to life. I just knew it couldn't be done. No-one can do that."

"Did you tell Dilys?"

"Yes. She smiled, rolled her eyes in the kindest way, and held my hand for a moment. But when I read on, I found there is actual proof that the crucifixion really happened, from historical sources who were neutral observers. Dilys said that Jesus chose to do all of it for you, for me, and for her. He got our punishment. It was personal."

"Why did he have to die?"

"I asked Dilys that exact question. She spoke about death. I recall her saying death made a nonsense of creation. Nobody makes things so that they break. She said Jesus had defeated death. But I didn't understand what she meant, and I still don't, but I so want to!"

"Did you discuss anything else, Harry?"

"There wasn't much time, Pete, but she did say that historically, the gospel message got hijacked and distorted as a behaviour management tool for those in power over the ordinary people. That made her angry. She knew it was simple, like when the first believers were around."

"Dear old Dilys, hey?"

Harry sighed. "She certainly believed that man had made a mess of it. Dilys explained that she often prayed for the misled. For her, across the centuries and the continents, man had twisted what God had said and done to suit his own needs. She had no time for religion."

Pete put on his puzzled expression. "Explain?"

"For her, religion was largely a set of man-made rules. She was sure that, sometimes, religion distorted the truth. People apparently speaking with unearthly authority and power, telling others what to do to earn eternal life, how to behave, but through those rules and regulations. She didn't think much of the religious authorities, as they are called."

Pete changed his look to one of managed perplexity. "So how did she think people could learn?"

"Pete, Dilys told me that God's simple message was only the start and that God reaches out to anyone who asks, makes Himself known to them. They discover the rest from the Bible. As a teacher, I know that you can tell kids a fact until you are blue in the face – and I'm not talking head tattoos – and they don't know it on the day of the exam. But if the kids have found it out for themselves, they know it for life. That's how she wanted it."

It was Pete's turn to take a drink. "That's pretty much her."

Harry drew breath and continued. "She loved the time when we were a small group meeting in Martha's lounge. We talked about everything, different faith groups, even wacky stuff we'd picked up at the evening class. Dilys didn't mind. She just listened and led us on. She was so pleased when we had to move to the scout hut. By then she had definitely moved us towards a proper exploration of Christianity, and eventually was leading us to discover new parts of the gospel story each time we met, with no rituals, no fancy dress vestments. Just what to her was the truth."

Pete brought the conversation back to practicalities. "What did she think about the scout hut really, Harry? I mean, was it really suitable?"

"I'll be honest, in the winter, she wasn't always quite so keen. She told me it wasn't the greatest place to bring new people, but she had a sense of humour. We'd be going in as the scouts were coming out, so she'd give me a cheery and vigorous two-fingered salute which was open to misinterpretation by the more precious in the group. She'd then give me a solemn 'dob dob dob' on the way out. But she did point out that Jesus didn't have a church building, that he made his disciples work stuff out for themselves, so we should do likewise. I guess the place was part of the journey she was taking us on. Simple message, simple surroundings"

"Do you still want to find something more comfortable with her legacy?" Pete's question was sincere.

Harry stared at his glass. "I'd rather boil my head."

CHAPTER 6

"Judy, I'm back." Roger's voice echoed through the flat. "I'm ok. Good fresh air. Well, air at any rate."

"Are you going to open the letter?" Judy was straight to the point.

"No."

"What did the first one say that was so bad? You said it was signed by someone called Jonah, and he was telling you to go back to the UK. Was there anything else? A surname?"

Roger relented. "No. It wasn't really a letter. A phrase and a sentence. Herbert, Mission Unaccomplished. Return to UK."

"I don't suppose Jonah left a forwarding address."

"No, you're right. He didn't even sign it. Just wrote his name in block capitals, like he addressed the envelope." Roger scratched his nose. "Just a weirdo, probably."

"And this new one looks like it's from the same

person." Judy already knew that but said it anyway. "I remember the first one when it arrived. It's a bit unsettling, isn't it?"

"We are not going back to the UK. Someone is trying to undermine what we are doing here. Mission unaccomplished indeed. That's precisely why we are staying. To accomplish it. I know we must." Roger set his face with determination.

"Are you opening the new one? If that's all, let's face up to it." Judy's tone was reassuringly gentle. "Together."

"I will if you want. I just don't want you having more issues running around your head than you have now. You know how you've been lately,"

Judy sighed. "Sorry."

Roger unset his face with equal determination. "Judy, you have always underestimated how lovely you are, and if you could realise, I would be so happy. There is nothing to be sorry for, but I do understand."

"Sorry." Judy looked down and smiled shyly in the way he loved. "Just open it."

He did. "Block capitals again, same message. Herbert, Mission Unaccomplished. Return to UK. This time it's signed by, let me see, Amittai."

"Signed by whom? Are you sure?" Judy enquired patiently.

"Oh, sorry. No, I'm not sure. I'm not certain that's meant to be a signature. Sorry, you were right."

"Don't you start apologising for everything!" Judy grinned.

"He's written his name in block capitals underneath his message. But no, it's not a signature. But look, Judy, we are not going back to the UK. Not for Jonah and not for Amittai, whoever they are. I will not allow us to be distracted from our purpose. Weirdos."

"Hmm." Judy paused for effect. "Why use these strange names?"

CHAPTER 7

Harry opened their next meeting with a question. "Do we need a new name? For the chapel." It was a week later. He had been waiting for Pete for some time. Pete had taken Harry's empty glass back to the bar and got a round in.

"I haven't slept too well since we last met. I've felt sad so much of the time." Pete's answer was indirect. "I can't get dear Dilys out of my head. I don't think we have worked her out yet. I want to know she would approve – fully – of what we do next. There was more to her than meets the eye."

"You can say that again. One special lady."

Pete was not to be distracted. "I just get the feeling that we are taking on more than the revitalising of the chapel, more than putting it back on its feet." He stared at Harry. "And it's something to do with you, my friend. But what? I don't know."

Harry recovered his poise. "I've given this a lot of thought since we spoke. We've lost our guide on the journey, right? So we need someone to do that, not a new building. Someone to lead the discovery of what Dilys referred to as the simple good news of the gospel in our neighbourhood. We've got enough cash to house and pay the right person for three years. Correct?"

Pete nodded.

Harry stared him straight in the face. "So where is that person? How do we go ahead?"

Pete was not to be distracted now, either. "My friend, you are right, but I believe we need to speak about Dilys first. I can't deal with recruitment issues until we have done that."

Harry studied his beer mat. "Shall I start?"

Pete shrugged his shoulders. "If you like. Why not? Tell me from the start. When did you first meet her? Was it in Liverpool?"

"Dilys moved into the area a few years before I did. I'd moved up from near Guildford, on my own. Everything had gone wrong. My mum and dad died in a head-on car crash with a drunken driver, my marriage broke down, my daughter sided with her mother, and they cut me off. Totally. I was so bitter, I just had to get away, but kept putting it off. I knew a lot of it was my fault, not just one thing, but over quite some time. One night I had like a voice in my head telling me to make a complete fresh start, you know, change my behaviour and my lifestyle. So, I resolved to be a different person if I could, you know, change how I was. Losing weight was the easy part. The rest was tough, but at least I overcame the worst things about the old me." Harry lowered his head and drew a deep breath.

Pete lightened the conversation. "How did you lose weight? I'm always trying to lose a few pounds. Did you take up jogging?"

"No. I signed up with Weightwatchers but even then it went wrong."

"How so?"

"They asked me to leave after I'd been going for twelve months."

"Why was that? Were you too thin by then?"

Harry grinned playfully. "No, they told me it was my one-year anniversary of membership, so I did the decent thing. I took a cake in."

Pete laughed.

Harry's face resumed a serious expression. "In fact, Pete, I was a changed man. I lost a shed load of weight, went cleanshaven, bought some new clothes, smartened up and got a job up here, not far from the Anfield football stadium. On my first day at school I got acute toothache, and they sent me to the nearest dentist. Dilys was the surgery nurse. I'm still on their books now."

Harry paused. "The rest will cost you a pint."

Pete took the empties back and obliged, treating himself to another sparkling water. He put Harry's beer in front of him. "You do seem to like your beer, my friend. You didn't include that in that new start, I assume."

"No. I needed something to get me through the tough

times. Anyway, back to Dilys. We got talking. We would talk about everything. Almost. And what I didn't say, she didn't ask, but I felt she understood me. It lifted me to feel that she knew me through and through, what made me happy, what made me sad. It was easy to open up to her. She was an energetic lady with a mind to match. She was from the generation before mine, and she became like a mum to me. It felt like she counted me as family. Even at the age I was."

"Were you interested in Christianity at this time?"

"No, Pete, I wasn't. I had too many issues. I escaped them by going to the pub. Listen, what's this to do with rebuilding the chapel? Nothing!"

"To the contrary, my friend, everything. What were those issues?"

"I was angry with God about my parents. How could he have allowed that to happen? I couldn't answer that question."

"Could Dilys?" Pete raised his eyebrows.

"No. But she got alongside me, helped me through. Then one day she told me she had received a message for me from Jesus."

"How did you take that? Did you believe her?"

"Well, I rejected it immediately. I thought it was rubbish. She'd been praying for me; she'd told me that. But I thought she was going doo-lally when she said it. Barking, in my view. But she insisted. And the message was to tell me I was going to be amazingly loved."

"What happened next?"

"I went to school the next day. The local vicar was doing the assembly. And oddly, or so it seemed, it was about unconditional love. Perfect love. Like a father has for his children, except that we've messed all that up, most of us aren't great examples of how to be a dad, are we? I knew my dad wasn't perfect, and I can promise you I was anything but. It made me realise how much we humans have distorted love, and how much us blokes could be doing better."

"What happened then?"

"I thought, that love's just for the kids. It's a story. And it's not for me. But the thought wouldn't leave me. I went home strangely angry. I rejected it again. I went out for some air, but the anger remained. Then I bumped into Dilys on her way back from work. I'm afraid I went to her house for a chat. I told her so much. Not everything, of course, because we men don't, but all the good moments, and without boring her with the details, I told her how I felt pain and guilt from years ago when things went wrong, and that those feelings wouldn't go away."

Harry reached for his drink. He gulped a mouthful.

"Take your time, mate." Pete leaned back.

"She told me again that Jesus had this overwhelming love just waiting for me. I knew it was exactly what my heart wanted, but I wouldn't allow my heart to hold sway over my head. Two days later I stopped fighting it and I somehow wanted to accept it, so I asked her how I could do that."

"How have things been since then?" Pete's brow furrowed.

"Well, like before bad things still happen, and I get it wrong, but Dilys promised that one day God would come alongside me. I just hope it happens soon. Dilys talked to me more, and eventually I joined the philosophy class. I heard nothing that came near to what Dilys was telling me. I was so glad when we started our own group. Pete, I have this feeling that I could discover a peace in my heart that I never had as a child, as an adult, as a father. Or it's like being outside a room where there's a great party going on. And it's impossible to understand it, but I need to find the door in."

"So, life went on?"

"Pete, where has the time all gone? Yes, I stayed at the same school till I retired and made new friends, then soon after, attended the chapel with you and it made me increasingly curious. Dilys was such a blessing to me in many ways, some of which I only realised later."

"Explain?"

"I think I'm coming back to this power thing I mentioned before, you know, that I was aware of in Dilys. Maybe this is a part of it, I don't know. But Dilys told me later that she had prayed for me from the day we met, she'd continued to pray for me and for so many others every day of every week. When she retired, she simply redoubled her efforts. She touched so many lives. Friends, ex-patients, strangers. It took me a while to work this out, but old Dilys really knew the power of forgiveness. It's not natural to forgive people, is it? I don't think so. In fact, I think the opposite is the case. It's much easier to become bitter. Anyway, people said she was an everyday evangelist, firstly through what she did, how she lived her life, and then through the words she spoke. She was a blessing to me, but I'm not sure how. She just was. And to others. She met so many people and stayed in touch. I wouldn't like to have seen her phone bill or her postage costs, she was constantly alongside so many people. Abroad as well as at home."

"You said a while back that Dilys had you running errands for her in her last few weeks. What did you mean?"

"Mostly the good neighbour kind of stuff. She wasn't that mobile in the end, so there were bits to do for her. Cleaning too. I thought she was going a bit odd, you know. She asked me to bring her my toothbrush. I did, she'd just got a new one for me, but I wondered what that was all about. I asked her. She said her old workplace people, you know, the dentists, were doing some research and needed it. But there was one task which was even more odd. I'm still doing it now. But that's not for now, Pete. I've got to run. Meeting a mate for a beer or two."

Pete smiled. "I didn't want another drink anyway. Harry, you've been more than helpful. Let me give this some thought, and I'll try praying about it. Dilys would have liked that. Then we'll meet again in a few days."

Chapter 8

Roger's mobile chimed in his pocket as he climbed the stairs back to his flat. The graffiti-adorned lift was out of action again. He stopped when he saw Jeanne's name on the screen. It was a text message.

"Roger, get it now. Judy's with me. She's just in the ladies. I've got a new one for her in my bag. I'll give her it as a present when she gets back. Text me when you've got it."

Roger ran the remaining flights of stairs, unlocked the door and made for the bathroom. He grabbed Judy's toothbrush by the handle, eased it into a plastic bag and replied. He was to the point.

"Got it."

The reply was immediate. "Come down. I'll be outside in five, with Judy. My handbag will be open. Put the item into it but don't let her see."

It wasn't a great place to leave a handbag open, so Roger hurried to see the two ladies arrive. The plastic bag and its contents were surreptitiously exchanged for his wife, whom Roger accompanied back up the stairs. Jeanne headed off, zipping the zip as she walked.

When Jeanne got home, she pulled out a scrappy piece of paper from under her bed, copied the address onto a small packet, and asked Yvon to post it. The address was in the UK.

Five days later, as Judy took a shower, Roger's breakfast was disturbed by the postman. The third letter had arrived.

"Leave it on the table. We'll open it when I'm finished in the bathroom." Judy's sixth sense had swung into action.

Roger waited, finishing his coffee. He slid Judy's beverage across the table and opened the letter as she came in.

"Similar envelope. Same block capitals. Same message. Different signature."

Judy picked it up. "Signature? If this is a signature, the person's named after Nineveh."

"Doesn't make sense." Roger's face wrinkled up.

"It does. Book of Jonah. This is all about names. We need to look into them. Look. Nineveh was a place. Amittai was a father. Jonah's father in fact, but a father. Jonah was, erm, Jonah. And what did Jonah do?" Judy raised a finger.

Roger's brow did not unfurrow. "Travelled by whale? No, seriously, he was told by God to go to Nineveh. He refused three times. So God took him there. He was given a mission to carry out."

"I think we're going to the UK." A new kind of relief smiled in Judy's eyes. "By whale if the flights are full."

"But what for? What's it about? And who's behind this?" Roger caught his breath.

"Jonah found out when he went to Nineveh. Maybe we'll know when we get to the UK."

CHAPTER 9

The first storm of the autumn was venting its fury on the Liver Building as Pete sipped his coffee in a glass fronted café near the Pier Head. Harry strolled in, leaving the door ajar and pulled his chair up. Pete watched the waiter dash to seal the resultant aperture, refuse further admission to the rainwater and reduce the newly introduced whistling sound to that of a mere exterior howling. Only then did he take the order for Harry's requested cup of tea. An uneasy peace returned.

Harry looked nervously at Pete. "I don't like storms, whether they are real or metaphorical."

"This one is real, but it will calm down eventually. Something's on your mind, Harry. I can tell. Shall we see if we can calm that one too?"

"Yeah, can you read me so easily? When we last met, I think I took us off piste, telling you my life story. I don't know why I did it, so may I apologise? You were enquiring about Dilys. Not about me. Please forget what I told you. It was too much about me."

"To the contrary, old chap, to the contrary. What you told me was something that remained on Dilys's heart since she moved here. The use of the legacy, and our next move, has to be founded on Dilys. That's what she meant by rebuilding the chapel. Build it from the inside outwards. And be constantly listening to God and to each other. We are going to restore the sense of purpose, give it a new urgency and relevance today. Your story reminded me of what Dilys would have called the workings of God, and she would say that it shows how God uses everyday events and everyday people to build his Kingdom."

"What about a pastor? Was Dilys suggesting we needed to find a leader with some training? Like an actual minister?" Harry scratched his head. "We are on a journey, Pete, a journey. We mustn't rule anything out. If she meant us to do that, we will be shown the right person. Definitely. Will it be an everyday kind of person?"

Pete smiled. "Oh yes. When we began to meet, Dilys got each of us to tell our own stories. She started where each of us was at. We spoke of the places where we were looking for meaning in life. It was wealth for some of us, friendships for others. Death and mortality in your case, Harry, if my memory serves me well. We were all really looking for answers to life's great questions. So we need to revisit all of that again, but this time from where we are now on our journey. We need to find at least three more members of our chapel who knew Dilys and who will be prepared to tell their story to others, just like you. Once we've heard them out, we will have a proper basis for going forward."

Harry waved an imaginary pen in the air as he gestured to the waiter. Pete glanced at him "Are you feeling ok? Did you just call for the bill?"

"Yes I did, and thanks. I'm fine. There you go, I got it for you. I enjoyed the tea. Thank you. And I think you are right. We need to use the people we already have who knew Dilys personally as the basis for moving ahead."

Pete paid.

Back in Paris, Roger glanced wistfully at the Eiffel Tower from his pavement café seat near the Chaillot Palace. Jeanne pulled her chair close to the table. "Did you say leaving?"

"I've been in touch with my friends back in Surrey. We've had these messages to go back to the UK, and Judy is convinced we should go."

"Are you?"

"If I'm honest, no. But there is something to be resolved. Judy thinks it is God calling. I'm not sure if it isn't some crank trying to stop our mission here in its tracks, even the devil at work. The devil always gets involved when mission progresses. But we are going back on Saturday week, for an indefinite period. I'll be saying the farewells on Sunday."

A gust of cold wind blew between them.

"What about us?" Jeanne snapped.

Roger raised an eyebrow. "Us?"

Jeanne shivered. "Yes, us. All the people you pastor. Your mission, remember? In France. What's going to happen to us? When you've said farewell."

"That's why I wanted to meet this morning. I want you and Yvon to step up. Can you lead things until they find someone new? You two are great musicians, you have the skills you need to preach, you know your Bible well. You've a real heart for the oppressed, for what the world sees as life's losers. You'll be fine."

Jeanne shivered again. "I'll speak to Yvon. But you're forgetting something. I'm worried about Judy. Is it wise for her to go back to the very place she was abused? It could set her back ten years. All those memories. God may be telling her to go back but I don't know if the doctor will agree. And we are so close to helping her make serious progress."

"Ok. You talk to Yvon. I'll talk to Judy. We'll meet here again tomorrow."

Roger's mind was in torment as he caught his train back to the estate. Jeanne was right. But Judy couldn't know why he had been meeting Jeanne secretly for some months now, after he had shared Judy's issues with her. What if the abusive father was still around? What if he found her? He shook his head, recoiling at the thought.

Judy knew something was wrong. After dinner, Roger sat by her and took her hand.

"What have I done?" she asked quietly. "You haven't changed your mind, have you?"

"No." He cut to the chase. "Judy, what will happen if your father finds you when we get back to Surrey? You've felt safer here in France, and you know you are so much less troubled than you were. Bravado is one thing, but foolishness is only a step from it. Darling, I'm so worried."

He never called her darling. Tears welled up in her eyes, then his. "There's something I have to tell you. Some time ago, I told Jeanne about your traumatic past, you know, the physical and mental abuse by your estranged father. I don't know why, but I did. She told me she knew someone who could help, a Christian friend who would pray for you. Jeanne called her a prayer warrior. So, I encouraged Jeanne to make that contact.

As it has turned out, this friend was led by the Lord to a practical way she could help, if she had assistance from Jeanne. Jeanne agreed, of course, although she didn't have much idea what her friend was doing. I've been meeting up with Jeanne recently as she did her part. We think God is behind this, and something good is going to happen. It's gone a bit quiet lately, but Jeanne is convinced it will happen very soon."

Judy wiped her face carefully, first one side, then the other. "Roger, please tell me exactly what's going on. I hate it when it's about me, behind my back."

Roger took her tissue and wiped his eyes. It wasn't the moment to mention the toothbrush. "I can't, Judy, because I really don't know. All I know is that we have to trust that God is with us in this."

"I'll be fine in Surrey, Roger. I'm older and wiser now. And that tight-fisted, fat, hairy, old drunkard of a paedophile hasn't bothered with me since the family split, so he's hardly going to meet us off the plane."

Roger was heading back in the direction of the Chaillot Palace. Jeanne glimpsed him as she emerged through the crowds and they returned to the café, staying inside to avoid the Parisian chill.

Jeanne spoke first. "Roger, what did she say? Are you still set on going back to the UK?"

"She's still angry, deep down, about her father. I told her the risks. But she's determined to do it, so I'm afraid we are going. Saturday week, we fly to Gatwick."

"Good. We do."

Roger's jaw dropped. "Sorry?"

"You heard. We do. We are."

"We are what?"

"We're coming with you. I spoke to Yvon. Roger, we're all in this together. If there's to be a healing for Judy, you'll need me there. I've arranged for a couple of trainee friends to stand in for us with our work here, I know they will bring good things to the people in our care. We will pray that God sees to that. But we're coming with you, and that is that!"

CHAPTER 10

November had arrived on Merseyside. A bitter wind was blowing. Pete was making his way back home with a sense of satisfaction concealed behind his scarf-protected smile. Three chapel members had agreed to meet the following Friday to present their own story.

Friday came. As Harry arrived at the scout hut which had served them as a chapel for many years, he thought it looked old and tired, even dingy. The central strip light flickered and yellowed the interior as he put the chairs out and waited.

Simone was first through the door.

"Evening." She nodded at Harry. Her voice betrayed a neutrality of interest in what was about to happen, verging on a lack of enthusiasm. "I've brought Martha with me; I hope that's ok." Martha was Simone's sidekick who went everywhere with her. Less forceful by nature, Martha could still be stubborn when she needed to be.

A large red clipboard, closely followed by the attached and briskly stepping Pete, was next.

"Jack's just down the road. And that's it. Hello Martha, hello Simone."

"I asked Martha to come. I hope that's ok. Old Dilys would have done so." Simone reiterated.

Pete grinned knowingly "Ah yes, I invited Martha, erm, as well." He and Martha couldn't avoid a simultaneous smug smile.

The former called to the figure now at the door. "Hi, Jack."

"That's breaking news." Simone whispered loudly. Jack didn't hear. Martha looked puzzled.

"What do you mean?"

Simone sighed. "You know, names can create ambivalence, like when people say 'Did you enjoy your bath, Matt?' Do you get it? Hijack!"

Martha sighed. "Who's Matt?" Martha had worked in a library and didn't take easily to ambivalence.

Pete attempted to close off the conversational cul-de-sac. "Do you think we should start with a prayer? Dilys would have prayed for us. We could give it a go."

Simone smirked. "Do you need a prayer Matt? There's another one."

Pete affected tolerance. "Shall I try and lead us? Even if I stay standing?"

Simone didn't flinch. "Yes, if you tell us why we're here. I'm not praying for anything I don't know about first. And Martha agrees."

Martha looked. Pete nodded patiently. "Ok. Old Dilys, as you call her, left us a legacy to rebuild the chapel. Not the building, the mission. You all knew Dilys and what made her tick."

"Made her tick? Was she a teacher?" Jack intervened. "In that case, what made her tick would probably have been a fear of an Ofsted visit. It would have been the same for you, Harry, wouldn't it? You were a teacher, weren't you?"

Harry pretended to shudder at the mention of this august educational organisation. "I was, Jack. And no, Dilys wasn't. Certainly not in that sense."

Pete continued. "We need to discern her wishes as to how we use her gift. So by bringing you together, we can hear each other's stories of Dilys and what she did for each of us, learn from it and work out the next step."

Simone looked at Pete. "You go first."

Pete smiled. He knew this was coming. "Ok. I worked in international settings where relationships were really important. Success came through teamwork, and teamwork was achieved by bringing people from different countries to act in a common purpose. It was great, really satisfying, when it worked. But it involved people of different cultures, different faiths, and that seemed to me to be an unnecessary problem created by religion. For me, religion was simply a barrier to business success. There were too many reasons to argue about it. I couldn't see why religion was necessary in the world.

From there, it was quite easy to see how wars started. So I blamed religion for that. And when I came across Dilys, I told her that. I was angry with God for blocking my business plans and for causing conflict."

"Did Dilys help?" Simone seemed doubtful.

"Actually, she did. She showed me how religion was not the same as faith, not the same as Christianity. I worked out that war and conflict start in the heart of one person and are therefore human in origin. God doesn't start wars."

Pete stopped. "That's me done. Can I try that prayer now before we move to someone else?"

Simone looked at Martha. "I wish he'd just get on with it."

Pete kept the prayer short and invited Martha to go first, but it was Simone who stood up.

"Leave that to me, Martha. I'll tell everyone. Dilys and I go back a long way. I am proud to say I have assisted her in her professional work and private life since she moved here. I want you to know that my advice was a constant and dependable source of help and support to her. She knew she could always ask, and that I would be ready with whatever she needed to know. I met her at the dentist's where she worked."

Harry couldn't help himself. "Well, Simone, I didn't know you were a dental healthcare professional yourself! I've learned something new today!"

Simone was not to be thrown off course. "My friend, professional advice comes in different shapes and sizes.

One doesn't need to pull teeth to know the dental pain of others."

Harry looked puzzled. "Did she put your words into practice, then?"

Simone tolerated interruptions badly. "She simply said that no-one counselled her like I did. I was proud of that. And for your information, Harry, I have always supported poorer people in every sense. I have befriended Martha here, a lady who is poor in quality of life. I see that she gets out regularly with me. She benefits from the stimulation I bring."

Pete smiled quietly. "And how would you describe Dilys, Simone?"

Jack butted in. "Dead."

Simone's face moved from scorn to disgust. She had little time for Jack in the first place, and this was beyond the pale. "Jack, you really are the pits, aren't you? You make me sick with your pathetic and tasteless attempts to be funny."

A smile played briefly on Jack's lips. He wasn't her biggest fan and he'd riled her as he wanted. Then he backed off, "Sorry, everyone, the black humour comes with the job I do. I was out of order." He performed a mock bow towards Simone. "Pray continue."

Simone did. "Dilys was a great listener. She was prepared to learn what she didn't know. She used what I would tell her to help others. And she came to the chapel whenever she could, so a real Christian."

Pete resisted the temptation to challenge the last

remark. "Simone, do you have one lasting memory of Dilys, something that was better, or sweeter, or more poignant, than all the others?"

"Well, there is one thing. I found that she had got a pensioner's free bus pass. Now I am not a snob, as you know, but I do have standards. I would only use the bus as a very last resort."

"May I ask why?" Pete looked at her.

"You may." Simone flashed a glance towards Jack. "One is never sure of whom one will be travelling with, is one? Never sure. But our dear friend Dilys had actually taken to using her pass regularly. I was able to intervene, but without much success. I did feel better after I'd said my piece."

"Did she explain her behaviour?" Pete was keen to know.

"Yes. She said she wanted to get into conversations about Jesus with the people she sat near. Complete strangers. Extraordinary. It wouldn't be tolerated where I live, I tell you."

Jack took on a pensive air. "Oh dear. My dear Simone, one feels sorry for one."

Pete moved swiftly to head off a conflict. "Thank you, Simone. Interesting."

Martha raised her hand. "There's more to tell, I think, Pete. Simone is being very modest."

Pete was diplomatic. "Maybe that's for another day, Martha. Now then, how about you, Jack?"

Before Jack could begin to tell his story, the scout hut

door – a red, metal job built for security – creaked open to reveal a lone figure outside.

CHAPTER 11

"**H**ello everyone! I'm Hamish."

Five pairs of eyes focussed on the new arrival; a fuller figure made more dominant by the uneven door frame.

"He doesn't look very Scottish. Doesn't sound it either." Simone whispered in a confidential manner to Martha.

Simone's new hearing aid meant that her manner was confidential, but the message wasn't.

"Don't judge people! I've told you before!" Martha had had enough. "Do you want him in a kilt and sporran? Carrying a portion of haggis? Doing a highland fling round the back row? Singing 'The Bonnie Bonnie Banks' from the scout hut rafters?"

Simone glanced at Jack. Jack's legendary subtlety and sensitivity led him to offer his own personalised greeting.

"Hoots mon!" he volunteered. "Welcome to the chapel, aye, where there's no moose aboot this hoose,

~ 65 ~

aye. You must be new round here, Hamish. Sit ye doon why don't ye?"

"Jack! For goodness sake! Please!"

"Just making the chap welcome, Simone. Keep your hair on. Speaking to him in his own language. It's a gift I have. I'm sure Hamish will be reassured that he will be able to communicate successfully with friendly people here."

"I'm not sure about that." Pete was ruffled. "Hmm. What brings you here, Hamish? We're having a meeting."

"I saw the light on. A couple of months back, I was looking around the area for somewhere to rent. I got talking to an old lady one Sunday morning – a Welsh woman – who saw me in the road here. We got chatting. She said she was a Christian, told me about this place. They'd just finished their meeting. I said I was not of the faith but admitted to a little curiosity about the God stuff, and she pointed me to the door here as a place I could find out more, in pleasant company. But if you're having a meeting, I won't hold you up."

"To the contrary, Hamish, you have arrived at exactly the right moment. Please join us. You are a godsend. And I mean it."

Martha pulled up a chair for the newcomer. Simone moved her own to retain proximity to Martha. She cleared her throat to speak, but Jack beat her to it.

"Whereabouts in Scotland are you from, Hamish? You don't sound very Scottish. Either way, foreigners are very welcome here."

"I don't want to disappoint, but I'm not actually Scottish." The Home Counties accent verified his words. "Surbiton actually. And it's near London."

Simone looked cross, despite approving the newcomer's received pronunciation of her native language. "Then why are you called Hamish?"

Pete decided on a tactical interruption. "Look, why don't we introduce ourselves? My name is Pete, and this is my friend and colleague, Harry."

"Alright. My name is Jack" said Jack, reverting to his usual, more local tongue.

Martha looked sheepish and put on her welcome voice. "Hello! I'm so pleased to meet you. You can call me Martha."

"Why, what's your real name?" Jack spoiled the moment.

Simone restored dignity to proceedings. "I'm Mrs Wilson. Why are you called Hamish, then?"

"Look, just call me Mr McDonald." Hamish was ready to move on. "I've recently moved to the area. I want to find out more about what goes on here, get to know you. The old lady said that it didn't matter that I didn't believe, then told me I'd be made really welcome."

Jack coughed. "Och aye, and I hope the welcome you have received has come up to scratch, Hamish!"

Hamish pursed his lips. "I have never before received a welcome like this one for sure. It's certainly different. Anyway, here I am. Even though I'm not Scottish. Is the old lady joining us?"

Pete looked solemn. "I'm afraid she's dead."

Hamish nodded slowly as he took it in. "The conversation we had was a bit odd for a first encounter. I mean, I'd never even met her before. She told me she wasn't frightened of dying. I wondered if she knew something that she wasn't telling me. She had a strange peace about her as well as a zest for being alive. I haven't been able to get her out of my mind. I mean, people don't like talking about death, do they? We seem to pretend it won't happen. Couples talk about buying a forever home. But forever it is not. The old lady talked about it like others talk about the weather. Did you know she was going to die when she did? Had she been ill? She seemed fine when I met her."

Pete lowered his voice. "It was all rather sudden, to be honest. No-one seemed to be expecting it, did they?"

Harry's voice seemed loud. "The only thing was, well, this. You know I used to do errands for her when she needed, don't you? She gave me one task to do, another for a few days' time, and another a few days after that. She said to do them even if she wasn't here. And then said she needed me to go to speak, a few days after the third task was to be done. Four envelopes in total, the last one addressed to me."

Pete needed clarification. "Were the other three to be posted?"

"Yes. Dilys's task reminded me of people on tv who are looking for new houses to live in."

"What do you mean?" Pete looked mystified.

"She wanted me to put my own stamp on them."

"And exactly what was in your envelope?" Pete's enquiry was genuine.

"Just a time and a date. And it's a week Saturday. I don't know what I'm supposed to say. I presume I have to meet someone. I suppose they'll tell me where I am going to speak."

"Have you done the first three tasks?" Simone loved a good mystery.

"Just done the third one this week. A message to send. Seems a bit odd now she's gone, but like Hamish found, there was something about Dilys that was different."

Hamish was unmoved. "She asked me where I was from. I told her, like I've tried to tell you. When she heard my answer, she didn't take the mickey out of my name, but she asked me to do a task for her too."

CHAPTER 12

Pete surveyed those present. "Jack, we were about to hear your story."

"Ok yes. Not too much to tell you, but here goes. I'm working for a funeral director these days, as you may know. It was the morning after a service I was attending. Tragic, senseless death, a young man, Christian, in a motorcycle accident. Dilys was a mourner. It was odd because she had a peace, almost a joy about her. She gave me some interesting answers and her address when I asked her why. I was so curious that I went to see her.

I remember it very clearly. Dilys peered vaguely at me standing on her doorstep. "Can I help you?" It was mid-morning and she was still coming to. She didn't know me without my working clothes – black tie and all that. I answered her. "Yes, actually, you can. My name's Jack. I was at the funeral yesterday."

Anyway, Dilys blinked at me before she spoke again. "I am so sorry. Tragic, the whole thing. Was the young man dear to you? Are you coping with the family in their grief and bereavement in the aftermath of the funeral?"

"No. I'm really fine with it all," I replied.

Then she fixed me with a stare. "Ah. Oh. Erm. Are you sure? Did you not get on? Were there family issues? Have you come for help with some guilt?"

It was my turn to peer, blink and stare. I said "No, I work for the undertaker. Not that there's been too much work lately. I'm only part time and unless we have a few customers each week, I don't get the hours. I'm supposed to be semi-retired, you see, but we need the money. The winter was a mild one, and even the usual flu epidemic didn't materialise, so, how can I put it, I was glad of the work. Anyway, you gave me your address."

She tapped her head and looked at me. "Ah yes. You carried the coffin."

I went on. "Yes. With some help, of course. Anyway, you said something when we were talking, you remember, before we drove away after the cremation, which I can't get out of my head. I've been to more funerals than most, you know, and I thought I'd heard it all. But you said that good people don't go to heaven just by doing good things. I was wondering where you got that one from? You're going to disappoint a lot of people if that's what you tell them. "And I meant what I said. So, everyone, that's how I came to be part of the chapel. To look for the answers to my questions."

There was a pause before Pete thanked him.

Harry stroked his chin. "Jack, you must have many questions about death, like most of us?"

"Good point. Not really, Harry. You have to laugh at it if you're in the undertaking business, like in any job. You have to treat it as a kind of game. You wouldn't survive it otherwise."

"That's ironic, Jack!"

"I guess so. We hear all kinds of stories about our clients – you know, through the eulogy, or just from the mourners. There was the bereaved elderly chap who showed he had not lost his sense of humour when he spoke during his feline-obsessed wife's funeral."

"How did he do that?" Harry's face was full of anticipation.

"He told the mourners that his wife had more time for the pet than for him. On her deathbed she hardly spoke to him. She passed away after the cat had had a massive stroke."

"Ha ha. Any others?"

"There was one deceased man who apparently used to always meet his best friend for lunch at the pub at 12.59 pm, because he liked one to one time."

Hamish laughed. "Nice one, Jack."

Jack proffered a thumb in the up position. "We got a few celebs in our time. We buried the bloke who invented the hokey-cokey. Took two and a half hours to get him in the coffin."

Hamish chuckled again. "The old chestnuts are the best ones, aren't they, Jack!"

"Then there's the wake stories."

Hamish was warming to Jack. "You made those stories up. But do you get invited to the wake, then? Is that normal?"

"It does happen, Hamish, yes. Usually in advance of the funeral, though occasionally after the crem when they think there are too many sandwiches and not enough mourners. The best one like that was when there was a good spread and money put behind the bar."

"Weren't you driving, Jack?"

"Well yes, we were a bit short on the staffing front so I got to drive the hearse. We usually take it straight back to base as soon as possible after a cremation, especially when it is in use again later in the day, but this time there was no hurry. I'd missed my breakfast that morning, so the offer of a few butties and a cake was tempting. I thought I'd leave it in the hotel car park, have a cup of tea with a bite to eat and then head back later."

"And did you?"

"No. The client's family put a drink in my hand as soon as I walked in. More followed. I ended up ditching the vehicle and looking at the option of a taxi home."

"Sounds wise, Jack."

"Well yes, until I found out that the reason there were not many attending was not that the deceased was short of mates, but the hotel had just been prosecuted for hygiene issues with the food. I'd parked the hearse outside the main door. Those customers who did come in looked rather nervous. Food orders plummeted but I was not in a condition to move it anywhere else."

"Did you just leave it there overnight?"

"I asked the manager if I could leave my company vehicle in the car park for the night. He didn't look at it, but seemed a responsible sort of chap. He just explained that as a general rule, he would suggest I could, but that he was aware of problems with joy riders in the locality. I told him that was unlikely to be a problem."

"Was that it?"

"No. He said that some customers had chosen to spend the night in their vehicle to counter the threat of having the wheels stolen. I couldn't say there wasn't space to stretch out, but nor did I want to see it up on bricks the next morning."

"So what did happen?"

"Well, things didn't end there. When I went out through the car park to the road where I could flag down a cab, there was a policewoman watching me. She came up to me, looked me up and down and said "You are staggering." So I looked at her and said "You're not too bad yourself." Next thing I knew I was in the back of the police car trying to explain the events of the day. Tricky."

"Come on, Jack, I'll buy the rest of the tale but I'm not having that bit. That's another old chestnut if ever I heard one. Any other thoughts? Real ones, I mean."

"Just when people leave a list of music for their own funeral, it's always wise to check it out before it gets played. There's a cheerful hymn called 'Colours of Day' which is upbeat and sends people out happy. It's fine for a burial service, but the chorus limits its appeal at the crem. 'So light up the fire, let the flame burn, open the door, let Jesus return'."

"Thanks Jack. That was very entertaining. I'm not sure how much to believe, but it's the way you tell 'em!" Hamish sat back.

Jack wasn't finished with questions yet. "There's a lot of people choose songs like Sinatra's 'My Way' for their last piece of music, aren't there? What do you think of that?" Pete's enquiry caused a whisper or two among the assembled.

"Fine when it works out. Sometimes the minister has to press the right button as the coffin disappears behind the closing curtains, and I've been there when the wrong track has come on from the CD. It's hard to stop once it has happened. 'Another one bites the dust' came on instead of 'Bohemian Rhapsody' and another had requested 'Shining Light' but instead, the vicar gave them 'Burn Baby Burn'."

"Thank you, Jack." Pete glanced around the table. "I'm already aware of Harry's story. How about you, Martha?"

CHAPTER 13

Martha stopped looking sheepish and smiled, nervously tugging at the sleeve of her pink jacket.

"For most of my career I worked as a librarian. I still do a bit. Most people don't have much to say in a library."

"That's because librarians always go 'shhhhh'." Jack was quick off the mark. "I once borrowed a book on how ships were put together. It was riveting."

Martha was silent, Pete encouraged her. "Tell us more."

"I've actually been a Christian all my life. My family went to church every week, and I was taught by good people. I made a commitment to follow Jesus years ago, but a few years ago now, I began to find I was losing touch with it all. I was bored in church, quite honestly. I blamed myself, of course, but in the end, I missed a Sunday service. I went shopping instead. And from that day, I haven't been back inside a church. But I still felt there was a voice in my head speaking to me, telling me to hang in there."

Martha scratched her forehead before continuing. "Then I met Dilys. She'd listen to me going on. She said she was inviting some people to her house for coffee and a chat, but I thought they could come to mine. Simone said I should mind my own business, but I am aware from the library that the, erm, type of folks who come in, often on their own, are looking for something more than they had in life. Mostly, that is some company, but sometimes they are seeking a meaning to their lives now they have stopped working and have time to think."

Pete smiled. "Books are beneficial, aren't they, Martha?"

Martha shook her head slowly. "Books are good, but they can mislead as well as lead, it depends what they chose. So I started to chat with them when I could, to help them find a book that met their needs. Being able to invite them to my home was the next step."

"That's where I met you, my dear Martha." The voice belonged to Simone. "I didn't borrow books, you understand, I bought them. I recall the day we became friends. I had gone into the library for research purposes."

"She was looking for the ladies." Jack thought he'd spotted a motive. "I guess you liked having people at your home to chat, Martha. It kept your library quieter, eh?"

Martha was not to be challenged frivolously. "I do think we can all see ourselves as God's librarians, if we wish."

Jack looked up. "Should we all wear our hair in a bun and a tweed skirt, then? I usually charge extra for costume work."

Martha grimaced at the unwelcome vision, then relented. Her tone was one of long-suffering tolerance. "Jack, before you ask, I was one of the best at going 'shhhhhhhh'."

"You probably were Martha. I guess no-one gushed when you shushed!"

The evening drew on. Shortly before closing, Pete made the case for seeking a pastor, using most of the legacy to pay a salary and to provide housing.

"We all knew Dilys in different contexts, but we knew her heart was to bring people to a place where their questions could be answered through scripture. Dilys cared for the poor, as you recall, but she isn't telling us to give her money to good causes."

Jack raised a finger. "Where was she heading, Pete?"

Pete paused briefly. "On our journey with her, she was moving us in the direction she felt we should go. Dilys wants us to find someone to complete her work. She is looking to us to see who God has in mind to step into her shoes. I propose we seek that person urgently."

He looked around the approving faces. "Right, let's do it. And right now, let's do what Dilys would have done and finish with a prayer."

Simone took a deep breath. "What for? Either you tell us or I don't say amen when you've finished. I'm not in favour of us having a leader who likes modern music so I'm not praying for that. And neither is Martha. Can't stand it."

Pete prayed anyway, then drew on his diplomatic past. "We meet on Saturday afternoon next week. We'll see where we are up to then. We all must pray frequently between now and then that God will point us to his choice. He's aware of our needs, and those of the people who may be attracted to join us, more than we are, even if we think we know better."

Harry had the last word. "That's the day I'm going to speak."

When he got home, Pete rang Martha. "Martha, I wanted to check you were ok after speaking to us this evening. You got a bit of a hard time from our friend Jack, I fear."

"It's fine, Pete. I'm a lot more robust than the way I come across. I've put up with Simone for quite some time now, and we're still speaking."

"What did you mean when you said that she'd been modest?"

"Pete, modest wasn't really the word. She seems very self-opinionated to many people, and they are usually right. She's very set in her ways. But she told me that she lost her husband just a year after they were married, to a rare form of cancer. I think she built this hard shell around her after that, so she would never be hurt again.

She is really rather vulnerable, which is why I try to go out with her when I can. She's quite bossy to me, but that's ok. It's her way of getting through life."

Pete hesitated. "I didn't know that. She's actually quite needy, Martha, no?"

Pete hadn't finished with his phone. Later that same evening, Harry's mobile rang. Pete's name was on the screen.

"Harry, sorry it's late. Had a brainwave."

"Did you? Are you sure? Last year you told me you'd had a brain scan and they hadn't found anything."

Pete acknowledged his friend's wit but moved on. "Harry, Dilys wouldn't ask you to speak. She'd have asked me. You don't normally like speaking in public, do you?"

"No."

"So she meant something else. She's lived around here a long time, right. Now, what do some older people call Manchester Airport?"

Harry thought. "Ringway."

"Yep. And, Harry, what did Dilys call John Lennon?"

"She called him all sorts of things, Pete. She wasn't convinced by his hair."

"I mean the airport."

"Ah. Oh! Speke!"

"You've got it. It is in Speke. She doesn't need you to do any talking, Harry, she wants you to go to the airport."

"So the other parts are a time and a date. There's the

~ 80 ~

name too – Herbert. It now makes sense. Thanks Pete."

"Goodnight Harry. Remember Herbert is a first name as well as a surname."

Over in Paris, a week of packing was out of the question. Roger insisted on focusing on his work, leaving most of the luggage arrangements to Judy. Jeanne and Yvon prepared a cabin bag each and a large suitcase, plus the latter's guitar. Roger booked all the flights from Charles de Gaulle to Gatwick, Judy making a similar suitcase arrangement for Roger and herself. They would need to come back for the rest when the mystery of the messages was solved.

"I do feel a bit like Jonah," he confided to Jeanne, "refusing to go where God wanted. At least where I think God wants me. I just know we haven't finished here. We'll see you at the airport in the morning."

Jeanne reassured him "You were doing it for Judy. Don't forget that. But yes, Jonah did that."

Saturday arrived. The Saturday. The Eldermen were met at the terminal by an excited Yvon and Jeanne.

Jeanne was first to speak. "Roger, Judy, the flight's been cancelled. Fog at Gatwick. I've spoken to the man on the desk and they've put us on another UK flight. Sorry but we had to be quick. We'll sort it out ourselves from there."

Roger nodded his agreement. "I'll ring our friends in Surrey and tell them we'll be late. At least we've got most of the day to get there. Where can we get to instead of Gatwick? Luton? Southend?"

Yvon smiled. "Liverpool. John Lennon Airport."
Roger threw a knowing glance at Jeanne.

CHAPTER 14

Clear cold skies had broken over the Mersey. The sun began to pick out the Lancashire coastline, theatrically lighting the landscape for those on a mid-morning plane into John Lennon Airport. Roger looked at his boarding pass bearing his full name. He stretched to turn behind to Jeanne and Yvon. "Do you think God would have used a budget airline for Jonah if there had been any around in those days?"

Jeanne partially agreed. "Maybe not Ryanair. But it would have saved the whale some indigestion when the trolley was up and down."

Roger thought for a moment. "Jonah might have had a bit more leg room in the whale, even if a window seat was unavailable."

Jeanne looked at the cabin crew making their way through the plane. "He probably wouldn't have had the chance to buy a charity scratch card either."

Roger looked with more than a passing interest from his newly appreciated window seat, leaning forward and obscuring Judy's view. She patiently waited in the middle seat for a glimpse of the city. Time passed. The Scouse accents of the cabin crew contrasted sharply with the smooth tones of the captain, providing a foretaste of Merseyside as they completed their final checks before taking their seats for landing.

The Eldermen were no strangers to budget airlines. Ten years on mission in France meant a lot of travel, and the prospect of reaching Surrey by nightfall did not worry them. There was a hefty bump as the Airbus touched, or rather, thumped, down. It was the cabin supervisor who spoke, the accent revealing his Scouse heritage as he firmly placed the blame for the uncomfortable landing where he felt it belonged.

"Welcome to the rather firm tarmac of Liverpool Airport where the local time is, erm, erm, an hour earlier than in Paris."

Today, everything seemed to be happening an hour earlier than Judy would have liked. Her husband guided her through passport control and baggage retrieval to the exit. She blinked at the dozen or so expectant relations and friends on pick-up duty. Behind them was a bespectacled man with a large font 'Herbert' sign in his hand. In a smaller lettering below, he had added the word 'Dilys'. Jeanne led the foursome to him.

"My name is Harry." He extended a hand of friendship to two perplexed guests and two who seemed relaxed. "Dilys sent me. I've brought the car. Which of you is Mr Herbert?"

Roger shook his head. "None of us is Mr Herbert. Would somebody tell me what is going on here?"

Jeanne shot a glance in his direction. He shook his head again.

It was Jeanne who continued "I haven't heard from Dilys for a few weeks now. I knew I could count on her though. Very reliable."

"You haven't heard? She passed away recently. It was a bit of a shock."

It was Jeanne's turn to be shocked. "Really? I thought she had been active in the last couple of weeks, I knew of some correspondence from her."

Harry lowered his eyes as a sign of respect for Jeanne's feelings before insisting. "So which one of you is really Mr Herbert? I was told to bring a card with that name on it. By Dilys. She even left me the flight number."

Before Roger could say anything, Jeanne squeezed his arm. "Trust me. Harry, thank you for meeting us. Herbert was a code, a signal to me. You won't need that now."

Judy pulled Roger to one side. "How did this Dilys know the flight number when we were on a different one, and we didn't know that till after she'd probably died?"

Roger stifled a yawn. "Think Jonah. When he went the wrong way, he was fetched back by whale. Let's just think that's what might be happening now. For whale, substitute aeroplane. Neither of them are exactly business class. Let's run with things for now. We'll find out soon enough."

Judy studied her crumpled boarding pass. "At least it's not Ryanair. I wouldn't have believed you if it was."

Jeanne smiled at Harry. "We need somewhere to stay for a week or so."

CHAPTER 15

A night in a waterfront hotel was followed by a dawn walk along the banks of the Mersey. Harry met them as they emerged from breakfast.

"Good morning. If you'd care to get in the car, I'll take you to the chapel. Pete's leading this morning. You'll like him."

Pete alerted the fifteen or so attendees in the chapel to the new arrivals.

"We've got four visitors this morning, and they've travelled from France. One is an old friend of dear Dilys."

"What are they called?" Simone did not hold back.

"All I know is that the English chap may be called Herbert."

Two minutes later, Harry entered, followed by his guests.

"He looks a bit of a Herbert, doesn't he?" Simone nudged Martha.

"Why are they here?" Martha whispered her question.

"No idea. Something to do with Dilys, I suspect."

"The young guy seems ok," Martha observed. "I wouldn't mind stamping his book. And he has a guitar."

"Martha, he is here to join our group, not as eye candy for an elderly librarian. Dignity, my dear, dignity!"

Pete felt prompted to open the meeting in the way Dilys would have liked – with a prayer.

"Father, we thank you for the safe arrival of our visitors this morning after their journey yesterday. Bless their time with us, we ask."

This was too much for Simone. She poked Martha's drooping shoulder. Her attempt to whisper her thoughts was less than successful. "I don't think we should pray for them till we know more about them." She surveyed the gathered people, who were still, eyes closed and heads bowed.

Pete looked across.

"Are you ok, Simone? Do you need some help?" It wasn't the first time Simone had heckled Pete, but a heckled prayer was a new one on him.

A few moments later, undeterred, Pete asked one of the guests to introduce the foursome to the assembled. It was Roger who stood up.

"Thank you for your welcome this morning. My name is Roger, not Herbert, as you may think. Herbert is an old family name. My wife Judy and I are missionaries in France. Yvon here, and Jeanne, are finishing their training with us near Paris, where we are based as pastors, so one day soon, they can further the work in that beautiful country. Yvon and Jeanne specialise in ministry through music, but they can talk as well!"

"Isn't Yvonne a girl's name? And missionaries in France?" Simone was incredulous. "Aren't they all Catholics over there? Why on earth are you working there? Is Africa oversubscribed then?"

Yvon said nothing. Roger was unflustered. "The name is spelt differently from the girls' version. As regards missionaries, what you say may have been true many decades ago. But the secular movement has been powerful, and the Catholic church grew old and tired, so France has been a mission field for some time now. So has much of Europe."

Simone furrowed her brow. "So what do you do in Paris? Isn't it cosmopolitan, like most capital cities are these days?"

Yvon glanced at her before speaking. "You will know that France has been hit by a major migration of refugees from war and persecution. Entire families have fled their homes, leaving what they had and what was left of their livelihoods behind. Many have come to Paris."

"No doubt on their way to the UK." Simone sat back smugly as Jack began to bristle at the perceived crassness of her words. He restrained himself.

Roger intervened. "Some, maybe. But all with needs. Basic needs. Our work has included befriending them, supporting them, working with the authorities to find housing, so much more. Teaching them French too.

These are decent people whose lives have been catastrophically affected by war. Trauma is a terrible thing, especially when it's kids and young people who have seen it."

Simone looked distinctly uncomfortable. It was Jeanne who continued. "We are giving them a real hope, the hope of the good news of Jesus Christ, just as we seek to do for all those we meet."

Jack carefully shuffled his chair backwards into Simone's leg, but he had a new agenda. "Roger, I've never really got what Jeanne has just said. I know that Jesus dying was good, in some funny sort of way, but why it affects me, I don't know. I know lots of stories about Jesus now, since I came to the chapel here, and I know he did some clever things, but I don't know why he did them, or why it should make a difference to me. So if you can tell me, I'll be obliged."

Simone pushed his chair firmly back to where it was and stretched out her freshly bruised leg. "I'm surprised you don't know that, Jack. I don't think the nice man will need to waste his time on you."

The chair hit the unbruised leg as Jack responded. Before he could speak, Harry had a question. "Roger, what is the most important part of the teaching in your work near Paris? I presume it is Christian. Is there one thing that strikes you especially?"

"Yes. That is something so important. It applies to me myself, my wife, Jeanne, Yvon, and all of us here."

"And that is?" Harry was curious.

"When we pray the Lord's Prayer, we pray for forgiveness, don't we? We each have a lot that needs to be forgiven, yes? We've all – everyone of us – got things in our past that we messed up, got wrong, sometimes badly wrong, and we are full of regret and guilt that won't go away. Yes?"

They all nodded. Harry became animated. "Some of us have talked a lot about this." Simone's assent was silent.

Roger continued. "We all have that guilt. We can pretend we don't, but it doesn't go away. So being forgiven is a wonderful thing. Agreed?"

Hamish shook his head. "I see what you are saying, Roger. Surely though, guilt is what you deserve when you do something that is criminally wrong. I can understand forgiveness from a victim who is generous, but I will not accept that it can be forgotten."

"That's the problem." The speaker was Harry. "We forgive, but we keep back a bit of it. We call it learning from the situation, and it changes how we see someone. We call it wisdom. But is it really? We can't forgive totally, we just can't."

Hamish looked unconvinced. "It's the penalty you have to pay. But I must say, when I've been told I was forgiven by someone I've hurt, it leaves me feeling a warmth towards them."

Roger waited until Hamish's words had sunk in. "But we don't just ask God for forgiveness, do we? We have a part of the deal too. We say 'as we forgive those who sin against us'. Does that suggest that we can't experience God's forgiveness if we don't forgive those who have hurt us too? Whatever they have done? I believe that God works through human beings, because that's what he's got on earth. His forgiveness is worked through us to others. And then from them. But listen, there's a power you need to discover before any of this, a power that comes from somewhere else. That power has been so important in my ministry so far, and it applies to me as much as to you. Only then can it happen."

Harry put his head in his hands. The mood was sombre. Pete waited again before resuming the meeting. "Roger, can you meet up with us later this week and talk some more? I just feel Dilys sent you here to get us all in the right place to revitalize our mission, and it begins with us. You seem to be a guy with some answers for us."

Roger surveyed the room. "Yes, of course, but I don't give answers. What I do is enable people to discover those answers for themselves through understanding what God says in the Bible. Will that be ok?"

"Yes, thank you. Perfect. Now let's sing together. I'm going to ask Yvon to choose a song he knows and lead us."

Yvon smiled shyly. "Of course. But first, let me sing to you, with Jeanne. This is my favourite English song, called 'Vagabonds'. It is for us all. Then maybe we sing some more songs you know."

Jack stared at him. "Yvon, do you just play the

guitar? Do you play other things too? It's only that I am interested in how music is made. I knew a chap who played a miniature traditional Indian stringed instrument which he used to look after children when their parents were out."

Yvon knew his music. "Was it a mini sarod?"

Jack shook his head. "No, it was a baby sitar."

A groan circulated through the hut followed by a few discreet smiles. One of them did not belong to Simone.

Yvon waited, then blinked. "I see. I suppose for me, coming from my Congolese cultural background, I have a well-developed sense of rhythm. But it's just my guitar now."

Jack was sharp. "Ok, another time, I'd like you to play your country's native small drums too."

Yvon was sharper. "I'm getting to know you, Jack. You want to hear me on the bongo from the Congo."

Jack grinned. "Yvon, you and I are going to get on fine!"

Yvon retained the shy smile throughout the song he had chosen. When he finished, Pete joined Harry. "It's been a very good day. I like what we've heard. In fact, it's perfect. There's much food for thought."

CHAPTER 16

Back at the hotel later that evening, Jeanne, Yvon, Judy and Roger were enjoying a drink in the lounge as Harry and Pete came in. Pete wasted no time once he had returned from the bar. "Cheers! Thank you for today. You all made a big impact on us with what you said and sang."

"No problem," replied Roger, "it was very much like what we do at home in France. It doesn't matter who you are or where you live, our common humanity brings the same issues to be resolved."

"Can we talk a little about Dilys?" Pete heard a hint of nervousness. "How did she manage to bring us together?"

"Interesting question." Roger brushed his ear with his sleeve. "We were heading to Surrey last Saturday from Paris when the flight was cancelled. Jeanne got us re-booked on a flight to the UK which landed in Liverpool. There, we found a man waiting for us who thought I was called Herbert. That was Harry. He seemed to be expecting us."

Jeanne looked embarrassed. "I was going to tell you this soon. I'm afraid I have done more than you think."

Roger nodded thoughtfully as the other four stared at her in expectation. Jeanne focussed on them. "The time is not right now for the whole story, but I can tell you something. And it involves Dilys."

Roger prompted Jeanne. "You and Dilys go back a long way, I think."

Jeanne nodded vigorously. "I knew Dilys from some considerable time ago. We got along straight away. She was bright, She had known tragedy in her young life. Even in those days she was a wise lady who knew the Lord and could apply his love to modern life. She was much older than me and I looked up to her. I remember her moving to Liverpool."

Pete looked at the others. "She liked Liverpool. She settled well here. Jeanne, what did Dilys mean to you in those days?"

Jeanne thought for a moment. "Dilys was always a source of strength to me, back then, when I met Yvon, and throughout our friendship. She knew what really mattered, she saw beneath the surface, deep down, in the heart of those whose paths crossed significantly with mine. She never judged me or anyone, you know, never. She seemed to assess a person's Christian walk, rather, and I would say she tried to see them as God saw them, not as we seem to do."

Pete shuffled in his chair. "What about in recent times, Jeanne?"

"Yes, well, a couple of years back, Dilys heard something about a person she knew. The situation was tragic, a breakdown of relationships. She felt that God was calling her to mend things and had a special purpose for her. She did some research – she was very much at home with a computer – and began to search for someone who had disappeared off the scene. As a result, Dilys began to think France had something to do with it."

Harry looked intently at Jeanne. "France?"

Jeanne looked him in the eye. "Yes, France. She'd had to speak to the police at the outset, it was so serious, so tragic. They came round to speak to her immediately. They'd asked her to call them back if anything new came to light. Dilys took this seriously, as she knew God's heart for truth, and she didn't rest on her laurels."

Pete smiled. "She could never be accused of doing that."

Jeanne agreed. "Yes, so Dilys asked me to pray for her in the project. She told me a few details so I could pray in, you know, a meaningful way for her. I did. France is a huge place but God is bigger. I got a feeling that I was meant to be involved. Weeks later, I realised that a person I knew had their own story which could have fitted the jigsaw Dilys was putting together."

Harry rubbed the back of his hand. "Jigsaw? What do you mean?"

Jeanne ignored the question. "I thought, you know, there's modern ways of tracing people. But we couldn't afford to cause any more hurt, or trauma, by raking over memories which were still so painful, so we had to be discreet. DNA is the key these days."

It was Pete's turn to look puzzled. "So where did this lead you?"

Jeanne looked solemn. "Well, matters seemed to be coming to a head. All I can tell you is that Dilys advised that we needed to be in Liverpool, the four of us. Yvon knew that. But Roger, I'm sorry, I know you weren't planning to be here. You were so set on going back to Surrey. So I bought plane tickets for Liverpool. The Gatwick flight happened to be cancelled, as it worked out, but somehow, you and Judy were always coming to Liverpool."

Roger grinned. "I expected something had gone on. Jeanne and I did meet up a few times as her end of things evolved, but Liverpool was a shock to me as it was to you, Judy."

Judy was lost for words, but only briefly. "Erm, ok, but those funny letters addressed to you in your full title, where did they come from?"

Harry coughed. "That was Dilys. She told me when to send them. I didn't know why. She gave me the dates to do it. It was to France, to what I assume was your flat. The names meant nothing to me, I'm afraid. Herbert Roger Elderman was what she told me. I'm sorry I thought you were a Herbert."

Judy laughed. "Why did she do the full title?"

Jeanne looked at her. "We used it as a code. I knew

who the messages were from as soon as you told me, Roger. I just couldn't tell you any more than I did, and I still can't."

"What is it with names?" Roger mused. "But I forgive you, Jeanne!"

"I think we might all need a drink," interjected Harry. "Pete, mine's a pint. Same as before all round?"

"A toast." It was Roger who raised his glass. "To strange and wondrous ways."

CHAPTER 17

Sunday. Scout hut. Pete opened up. Harry arrived, bringing the France contingent. The chairs were out. As was Yvon's guitar.

Simone preceded Martha by a few seconds, took one look at the instrument and challenged the singer. "I trust you're not going to sing that awful song again, the one about thieves, abusers and murderers being on God's invited list? Preposterous. It was most inappropriate to decent people like us."

Yvon was taken aback by the outrage, she summoned up the courage to speak. "Simone, yes? I am sorry you do not like this song. Can you say why this is? You don't like the tune?"

"No, that's not it. The words are the problem. It's bad enough imagining heaven with rough people in it, but when you sang of inviting criminals of all kinds including the worst imaginable to be there, I'm afraid that was too much. It can't be heaven if there are dreadful criminals there."

Jack's head appeared through the doorway as Simone was speaking.

Pete cut her short as Jack moved to a seat beside her. "To the contrary, Simone. I have asked Yvon to sing it again. We have a Bible reading about a man called Zacchaeus, and Roger has promised to say a few words about it."

Simone was cross. "It'd better be worthwhile. Otherwise you may find that Martha and I may not be staying till the end."

Jack nudged her. "Did I hear you say rough as I walked in, Simone? Rough people in heaven? Do tell!"

Simone decided to make an effort. She sat forward and began. "I know you don't like me but I've always tried to be a good person and I consider that my faith means everything to me. I like to think I have always had a heart for the poor in all I have done in my life. And by that, I mean what I call 'the poor in spirit', as I find the term 'the great unwashed' to be demeaning. So I have done my bit for rough people, but I'm not sure criminals should be in heaven. That's who hell is for."

She looked at Jack. Jack shook his head. "Sorry, Simone, you are out of order there. Well out of order. Again. What you say doesn't show in who you are. My Uncle Bill was one of 'the poor in spirit' when he ran out of Johnnie Walker."

"Jack, I mean those who don't have much fight in them. People who don't make much effort in life."

"Unlike you, eh?" Jack shook his head again and

grimaced. "In my house we used to call my neighbour 'the exorcist'. One visit from him and all the spirits were gone."

Simone was exasperated enough to stand up as if about to leave. Martha shuffled in embarrassment. It was Hamish who sensitively intervened.

"Does this area have a lot of poverty among the people here? I mean real poverty, not just superficial." His voice was soothing and his question genuine.

Simone sat down again as if reassured. "Ah, Mr McDonald, forgive me. I'm forgetting you are new to the area. Yes, it's pretty rough out there."

Jack had the bit between his teeth and was not letting go anytime soon. "Yeah, it's rough alright. What Simone means is that not all of the people can afford to buy their food from M&S. Poor thing, she has even had to sit at the chapel with some locals who only live in semi-detached houses. She crosses over the road to avoid people from social housing."

Simone subsided. Before she put her head in her hands, she muttered. "He's horrid. He's a bully. I hate people like him."

Pete tried to draw a line. "Come on you two, you can do better than that."

Jack ignored him but decided to lower the level of his invective. "I've been a working man all my life. I've known rough times. I had a spell on the bins which wasn't great." He paused to look at Hamish. "It was a rubbish job."

Martha grinned. Simone elbowed her in the ribs. Jack went on. "I was in and out of work, then ended up working for an undertaker. As you know, I still do a bit now. Dead end job."

Martha grinned again. Hamish smiled at Jack.

Jack was done. "Sorry, Simone. I shouldn't have said that. I can't help myself sometimes."

Simone sniffed. "You're just rough."

Jack looked at her. "I'm rough, I guess. I've done basic jobs many people won't do. And I have done stuff in my life which I shouldn't have done. I guess that makes me a criminal. But it feels like you are judging people, Simone, I'm sure of it. What you wear is not who you are. I wore jeans and a tee shirt when I came to the chapel the day after my Dad passed away. I didn't dress up, and I haven't since, except when I'm on duty, embalming and coffin bearing. Despite everything I have done, despite the way I dress, almost everyone at the chapel has made me welcome. Dilys said you would."

"I presume your Dad was a believer, Jack. Was he a churchgoer? Is that how you knew you would be welcome?" Hamish's tone was quiet.

"No, Hamish, far from it. Dad never believed in any of this religion thing. He said it was the cause of too many wars to be real. I knew what he meant but I thought, well, there must be more than that. So Dilys got me to come here, I came back a few times and I've felt welcome. Even though I'm rough."

Simone pointed at Hamish. "Why don't we ask Mr

McDonald? He's newer than Jack." She didn't wait for an answer before turning to the startled man. "What's your view, Mr McDonald? You've experienced our welcome at first hand, haven't you? Do you think criminals should be allowed into heaven?"

Hamish raised both eyebrows. "To me, Simone, you seem very much part of this group. And so does Jack. Draw your own conclusion."

Jack began to be conciliatory but couldn't keep it up. "Ok, I accept she's just posh. Even her food is posh, you know, she even eats that vegan stuff. I hope that's not on the menu in heaven." Jack threw a sidelong glance in Simone's direction. "And I hope they're not all like her in heaven. Perhaps they won't let either of us in."

Simone could not resist it, attempting to claim the higher moral ground. "I'm sorry, Mr McDonald, that you're being dragged into this. Jack found out a few weeks ago that I had recently become attracted to a vegetarian diet, and he hasn't been able to deal with that very well. The man has no sense of sensitivity."

Martha was enjoying this. "Almost a book title, Simone. Jane Austen." She glazed over. "However, your memory is slightly off beam, Simone. You turned to vegetarian food in the light of the incident at the community Summer Sausage Sizzle. When we did a Chapel hot dog stall to try and get better known in the neighbourhood and Jack took charge of it."

Simone shuddered. "That was dreadful. Why he was allowed to do a 'sausages of the world' theme, I have no idea. He waited till I had tasted the Korean sausage he offered before telling me the hot dog I was chewing really was what it said. Dog."

"I was only joking," commented Jack. "It certainly got us better known."

"Yes. So much better known that no-one came near us. People love their pets. They were so offended. And so were we."

"It was your fault, woman. You just over-reacted. You screaming and spitting out my Korean sausage didn't actually pull the crowds in."

"I had to get it out of my mouth. You disgusted me. I felt physically sick. If that was supposed to be funny, it was a disaster. No-one knew you were joking, and you know what? I'm still not sure."

"It wasn't true," confirmed Jack. "It was Vietnamese."

Simone exploded. "Get him out of here. He's foul!"

Some minutes later, Pete brought Jack back in. Simone had recovered her natural colour. Jack looked her in the eye. "Sorry. I was out of order."

"Friends, shall we move on?" Pete's melodic tones ensured closure.

CHAPTER 18

The time for vitriol was mercifully at an end. The format of the session settled them down after the unstructured and unplanned exchange of unpleasantries. Harry was asked to read the Bible story of the tax collector to the assembled, Yvon sang the song and Roger began with a question. It was not rhetorical. "How do we feel about tax collectors? Do we value them today?"

"Can't say I'm over keen." Jack was first off the mark. "Let's ask Hamish. The Scots are good with their money."

Hamish sighed. "Jack, I'm not Scottish. Never was. Never worn a kilt. Have you?"

For Simone, this was a vision too far, but before she could speak, Roger reversed the conversation out of the dead end. "You may know that in Jesus's day, the Romans were occupying the land. Their army had taken over, like Hitler did in France. The tax collectors were hated because not only did they collect money from the

Jewish people to give to the Romans, but they also extorted as much as they could from ordinary – including rough – people for themselves. They were the scum of their time. Like people traffickers or drug dealers today. Zacchaeus was one of them. He wanted to see Jesus so much that he climbed into a tree to get a good view. How did Jesus treat this scum?"

Simone had been listening. "Someone here would be telling you that if Jesus invited himself for tea to my house, I would only let him in if I had some Earl Grey in to serve with the petit fours. But Zacchaeus would have been amazed, wouldn't he? I hope he had some decent provender to set out for his divine guest, though."

Roger nearly smiled as he tried not to sound patronising. "I'm sure he did, Simone. But the point is that Jesus socialised with scum. Made friends with them. Need I say more?"

Yvon took his chance. "You see, everyone, forgiveness cannot have boundaries, like the song I sang says. Everyone can be forgiven. That is why the song is so important to me. And we must find the power to forgive them."

Pete recalled Dilys's example. "Our dear friend Dilys knew that. She said when Jesus died to pay the price of sin, he did it for all sin, not just the ones we think are less serious. Salvation is for everyone if they ask for it. Dilys made it her mission to make that known. Even murder, genocide, you name it – and child abusers too."

A phone alarm buzzed. The door of the hut opened,

and Hamish was gone without a word. The meeting ended quietly with a familiar song, and Martha served the coffee with help from Harry.

Pete clapped his hands. "Listen, everyone, we've enjoyed having our visitors for the last two weeks. They have challenged us to look more to God, to be kind to others rather than judgmental, and above all, to forgive others so we can also be forgiven. God sent these folk to us through Dilys, I'm sure of it. She has made us a financial legacy to rebuild the chapel. I'm going to ask you if you feel that you have heard something in the last fortnight which points to us asking someone here to become our new pastor. Do pray about it. So long as it's not Jack." Jack waved cheerily. Pete made a hand gesture to acknowledge him. "I'll be ringing round you all later in the week."

Jack stayed in his chair. When the others had gone, he put his hand on Harry's arm. "Harry, have you got a minute?"

"Yes, what is it, Jack?" Harry sat down beside him. Jack was not in his comfort zone.

"Harry, there's something I need to tell you. We were on a job a couple of days ago. The journey took us through town. It was late morning. I was driving the limo, slowly as usual, then I hit the red light at those roadworks on the way to the church, a couple of hundred yards before the school. That's when I saw Hamish. He was coming down the path from the school entrance, then he started to hang around outside the gate."

Harry smiled. "Ok, so what's wrong with that, Jack?"

"I don't imagine there's anything in itself. But if you think that Hamish isn't from round here, you could ask why he was loitering outside a school."

"Jack, did you see what kind of a school it was?"

"Yes. I could see the notice board outside. It was a secondary school. Why was he there? I don't know."

"I've no idea either. Maybe it was by chance and he was just waiting for someone, you know, nothing to do with the school."

"Harry, I'm worried it was a bit more sinister than that. You don't hang round a school, do you, unless you are waiting for someone in it. And the school lunch break wouldn't have been far off."

"Do you think he was waiting for one of the kids, Jack? Are you thinking Hamish was up to no good?"

"Harry, he seems like a decent bloke to me. But then I remembered reading that people who groom kids on the internet often seem to others to be decent people. I'm not accusing him, but I, erm, I don't know what to do. Maybe nothing."

Harry interrupted quickly. "Are you suspicious, then?"

"I'm just very uneasy. I can't get it out of my mind. There's more too. I was stuck in the traffic queue for a few minutes before I got through. I saw a police car in a side street. There was an officer in it. He seemed to have his eyes firmly fixed on Hamish."

Harry's face wrinkled up. He was also outside his

own comfort zone. He thought for a moment. "Jack, you are right to be concerned. Crimes against children are appalling and we must all guard against such things. But did the officer make contact with him? Speak to him? Arrest him?"

"Not while I was watching. But as I moved off on the green light, I saw an adult come out of the school who spoke to him briefly. This adult waved to attract the attention of the policeman in the car. The car came round to the front of the school and then he took them both away."

"Which school was it, Jack?"

"The one not far from the dentist where Dilys was employed."

"I know it well." Harry hesitated. "That's where I worked. It's got an excellent reputation, despite that!"

The smile was back on Jack's face. "If they had arrested him, he'd be Jock in the dock, eh, Harry?"

"Well he was here a few moments ago. We could have asked him. Maybe he's on bail, Jack. I guess that's a possibility. Was the rest of your day ok after the school incident?"

"I worried about what I should do. I even tried to pray, but I'm not sure anyone was listening. Maybe I used the wrong words. But I feel better now I've run it past you."

It was after seven in the evening when Harry and Pete met up with Roger in the hotel bar.

"Pete, Harry, I've asked Yvon and Jeanne to leave us

alone for a few minutes. And Judy will be along soon. Hamish called in and asked to speak to her, so they're talking in his car. However, the point is – and I'm so sorry to tell you this – but I'm not sure we are able to do what you are going to ask us. I'm not feeling it." Roger was to the point.

"Ok." Pete seemed to ride through any disappointment. "Can we do one more thing? See if anything becomes clearer? I haven't got around to ringing anyone yet."

"We leave on Thursday. What can we do for you?"

"Tuesday evening. There have been a lot of questions raised by our people since you've been here, and we haven't done anything with some of those. They need to find the answers. These are vital issues if Dilys's dream of rebuilding the chapel is to be achieved. Unless those we send out into the community are on the right song sheet, we just won't do it. Will you bring Yvon and Jeanne with you, and put on a session where we sing some joyful songs together and tackle the rest of the questions?"

"We will. But we'll book a room in this hotel for the meeting. We need to feel comfortable. Can you excuse me for five minutes? I have something I need to do."

Roger went up to his room. Jeanne was waiting on the landing. "News. We're nearly there, Roger. The test is due to take place shortly. The results are due to be with the dentist on Thursday by mid-afternoon. But we don't know where the dental surgery is exactly."

"Jeanne, I know a man who does. He's downstairs. Leave it to me." A look of alarm suddenly crept across his features. "We don't have much time left. That's the day we're leaving."

Harry was only too happy to agree. "Sure, Roger. I know the place well. I'll call in there for you."

CHAPTER 19

Monday dawned crisp and fresh. It was time for a day off. First, though, there was an unexpected interruption. Hamish walked through the door and came towards their breakfast table. Roger stood up and they moved into the corridor.

"Just touching base before I go back. When are the test results in?"

"They're sending an e-copy on Thursday afternoon. The receptionist will print it out and seal it in a blank envelope. Harry's picking it up for us."

"Roger, that is a vital document. What time exactly? Any idea?"

"I thought we'd get him to go around 3pm."

"Is he going on his own?"

"Yes, he's very reliable. He's known at the surgery too as he's been a patient there for some time. Hamish, we mustn't do anything to disturb the routine of the community on this issue, it's too sensitive. Harry must be in the place, alone."

"Roger, that's tricky. He must have someone with him. Or I could arrange something else which would work."

"Do that, Hamish. Where are you off?"

"Back down south to tie up the loose ends. I'll be back Thursday lunchtime, as it happens."

Hamish waved to the others and Roger re-joined them. The waiter brought him a fresh coffee.

Jeanne watched him take a first sip before she spoke. "Judy, I haven't been quite straight with you recently, and I'm sorry. To make up for it, I'd like to invite you on a cruise."

Judy was stunned. "Jeanne, we can't accept. A flight on a budget airline is one thing, but a cruise? No. Anyway, there's no time."

Jeanne grinned. "Just trust me. It's all sorted."

The Mersey ferry pulled out on the 11am river excursion. A dozen or so hardy ancient mariners on concessionary tickets were with them as they headed north. A solitary pursuing seagull stood in for the requisite albatross. The strains of Gerry Marsden singing 'Ferry Cross The Mersey' wafted on the stiff maritime breeze. Yvon looked at the distinctive buildings lining the river and raised his eyes to the Liver birds. "You know what? I just love this place. The people, the music, the humour. I've begun to understand the local accent too."

"That is quite an achievement," Judy chipped in. "I have trouble."

"The waiter taught me a few words of, how did he say? Yes, scouse language. Apparently, he liked my kecks."

Judy screwed up her nose. "What are kecks, for heaven's sake? I dread to think."

Yvon tugged at his trousers. "Perhaps I can ask Jack to teach me some more."

Judy frowned. "Yvon, when you get around to writing in English, please don't put these in your worship songs."

Yvon looked at her. "Certainly not the kecks, Judy. I promise."

The following day, Pete's efforts to bring the group together had been successful. To Jeanne's delight, the hotel had provided a warm and welcoming room with comfortable chairs, arranged in a circle. Of the promised attendees, only Hamish and Roger were absentees. It was Jeanne and Yvon who were last in, following Judy through the lobby. Pete looked content, but Harry had a grin from ear to ear.

"What's up with you, Harry? You look like you've backed the winner in the Grand National!"

"Sorry Pete, but I just got the wish I expressed when I heard about the legacy! It feels like Dilys has provided us with a modern place to meet after all. Luxury, I tell you."

A hush descended. Jeanne stood in front of the eagerly awaiting group and offered Roger's apologies. She explained that he had given her the task of speaking to them all, but had hoped to be there to listen in. However, an urgent matter had come up and he was hoping to get along later but had asked her to start without him.

She did. "May I be blunt? I am so pleased we can experience meeting here in this hotel. I would encourage you to do this when you have a meeting where you bring interested friends along. In France we talk about meeting people in their comfort zone, and, great though it is for our usual purposes, a scout hut isn't anyone's comfort zone. Not with the chairs you've got there! Our great friend Dilys would approve of planning to do this as you go forward, I promise you."

She then asked Yvon to open the meeting with a song. "You will need to listen hard. Remember Yvon can be limited in his English!"

Yvon, who had not wasted any time to improve his English during the stay on Merseyside, glanced up from tuning the guitar. "Yer wanner bet?"

Harry didn't miss his chance. "Yvon, you're going to be an honorary scouser!"

When the appreciative applause and laughter died down, Jeanne continued. "I prefer the songs which contain Bible teaching, because we remember songs, don't we, often word by word? We can't always recite the sermon after a service, but songs – we can do. Especially choruses." A murmur of concurrence rippled through the room.

Simone spoke up. "Jeanne, have you made us

comfortable so you can deliver a long sermon then? I do hope not."

Martha looked on apologetically. "Simone means well. It's just that we prefer to be informal."

Simone wasn't having it. "I do not mean well, I mean what I say. We don't do services and we don't do sermons. We meet. I have friends at churches who sit through some long ones till they are numb."

Jack couldn't resist it. "Numb bum syndrome. I know what you mean. Occupational hazard in my job. Gets you on both cheeks. Repetitive strain injury if you're not careful. You can probably sue someone for it these days."

Simone was not for stopping. "Over an hour at times. I mean, people have their lives to get back to on a Sunday, don't they? It's a bit rich."

Jeanne smiled patiently. "Understood, Simone. Dilys preferred discussion and discovery, not didactic teaching. I know people like me can go on a bit. But if we feel that God is leading us in what we are saying, it is hard to stop."

Simone was brutally frank. "You'd stop if we followed my plan. We should so do what Hamish did last time. Just walk out. Had enough – clear off."

Jeanne smiled again, a little less patiently. "Have you ever been invited as a guest to something really special? And when you arrived there, they were waiting to welcome you, and there was a place for you at the table for a beautiful dinner? I would like to share something today about how that welcome is out there for you, in a home where you can find both love and grace. But it is not a home on earth. The host is simply waiting for your RSVP, and he wants you to be there, whatever your past. Even if you feel like a bunch of vagabonds."

"That's no way to address your friends!" Harry gave her a grin. Jeanne did not return it. She'd had enough.

"Harry, my friend, I'm afraid it is the way. It really is."

There was a pause, a reflective silence. It was left to Jeanne to break it with an invitation to stand in prayer before she led them meaningfully. "Father, may you give us patience as well as eyes to see and ears to hear. We seek your wisdom on these issues for which we ask greater understanding. Now we only know a fraction of your greatness and see only glimpses of your power, and we need to know more. Teach us and empower us, Lord, as we seek to understand your wonderful invitation. Amen."

Jeanne invited the gathered to take a seat. "Let's set out our agenda. You have come up with some great questions we need to answer. There are five topics we have picked up. Number one, why good people don't go to heaven, number two, why bad things happen to good people and number three, why God allows war, murder and other terrible events. Number four is about judgement and who can be forgiven, and number five is what the Bible teaches about death. And you probably have a few more too which we might have missed."

Simone, slightly subdued, raised her hand. "Can we ask questions as we go along?"

Jeanne sipped from her water bottle. "Yes, Simone, of course. I promise you this is not a sermon. But there is a cross-over in some of the areas we may be looking at, so hear me out, if you please."

Simone slowly nodded. Martha sat at her side, her gaze fixed on the speaker.

Jeanne began. "On a practical note, can you check you have the wifi for the hotel so you can check Bible references on your phone?"

Simone looked at her in consternation. "Jeanne, I hate mobile phones. Can I use the traditional book version? I've brought it."

"Simone, that's fine. Now let me start by saying that we have loved our time among you since we came to Liverpool and met you all. Your issues have become dear to my heart. I have things to put to you which may help you as you resolve matters. Our agenda tonight is some kind of fusion of your issues and my thoughts for you to consider, in the light of Dilys's heart for God. So where shall we begin? What was the first question Dilys raised with you when you were first meeting, or even chatting with her?"

Pete's face lit up. "It was about ways we know for sure that there is a God. Dilys started by speaking to me about creation, and I guess that was true for us all. Am I right?"

The others nodded. Jeanne too. She lowered her voice

to command their full attention. "Let's take that one first, shall we? It really is a chance to begin at the beginning, if you follow my meaning. The Bible tells us that God created the world. No man could do that, no army, no organisation, no scientists, and certainly no politicians. But God did. God exists outside time. And the creation was good. We can all see the beauty of God's creation when we look around our region, our country and around the world."

Martha raised her hand. "That is true, Jeanne, perfectly true. But what about when it's not beautiful? Hiroshima, violence, hatred. Where does that fit in?"

Jeanne shook her head. "Awful. Martha, simply awful. In every part of life we also see that not all is well, and sometimes it is appalling. Everywhere we see bad things happening, damage done to what has been created by God, ugliness, sickness, and of course death."

Martha stared at Jeanne. "So can you tell me where all that does fit in? How come God allows that to take place if he is all powerful?"

Jeanne paused a moment and then continued. "Yes, that doesn't make sense, does it. How can it be that a mighty and loving creator God should allow that to happen to his handiwork? Something must have gone radically wrong."

A male voice interrupted apologetically. It was Jack. "So what was it? And how do we know that is true? What proof is there? Is it in the Bible?"

Jeanne was ready. "That's actually my next point, Jack."

"Sorry, Jeanne, it's just I need evidence. I want to believe stuff, but I'm the sort of chap that needs to be sure."

"Jack, you are going to like Thomas, I suspect. The disciple who wouldn't believe the others. He was exactly like that, he had doubts, didn't he? But I think we all do. And I have evidence for you. Can I take you to the story of Adam and Eve – whether you think it is a true story or a picture to help us understand? There, we see Eve being tempted by the devil. Adam and Eve then commit a sin. A sin is an action or words that go against the wishes, purposes and love of the Father.

Towards the end of Genesis 2 and onto the third chapter, you can see how Adam and Eve are together in the perfect world, but then defy and rebel against God, and the promised consequences then have to happen. The creation was broken because man, through Adam and Eve, rejected the creator and thought they could be equal to God. Take a moment to look at it now. Read how perfect it was in that second chapter, then see what happened in the next one 3, from verse 1."

The room fell silent as they read the passages.

Jeanne waited until expectant faces were raised towards her before speaking slowly and thoughtfully. "Is that you? It is certainly me. How many times do we wonder what God is doing about a situation, or a person? You see, we think we know better, don't we? And we forget that God is the almighty creator who lives outside time who loves us beyond our understanding. We dare to question him. Us. Humans. Made by Him to be his children. Yes, children."

Harry shuffled and looked up. "So, we are invited to be in God's family, I guess."

Jeanne took her chance. "I know some of you have concerns about family problems in the past. Let's think about human families first. We have heard a lot about fathers these last few days with you, both in our discussions together and in private, and our world does not always offer great examples of what a loving father really looks like, does it? Even the best human fathers are flawed. We are not exactly in a strong position to challenge the perfect father of creation, are we, Harry?"

"I don't feel that we are, Jeanne. No. May I ask one more question? It's no secret that I enjoy a beer. Maybe more than one. Does God approve of alcohol? Or is it wrong?"

Simone tutted. Jeanne raised an eyebrow in her direction but Simone said no more.

"Jesus drank wine, Harry. But not to help him deal with life. Do you drink to enjoy it, or to avoid answering life's hard questions? That's maybe something to ponder. Have you got it in the right context?"

Harry stroked his chin thoughtfully. "Hmm. Thank you."

CHAPTER 20

At that moment the door to the room slowly opened. Roger strode in, followed by Hamish, whose gait was hesitant and whose eyes were fixed on the floor.

Jeanne affected relief. "Great, Roger can help with these questions now."

Simone shook her head. "Jeanne, please keep going. I'm so with you."

Roger sat down by Hamish.

Jeanne picked up where she had left off. "Can we see something else in the story of Adam and Eve? Can we see justice?"

An air of enquiry filled the hotel room. One Bible was leafed whilst online versions were searched, but this time Jeanne did not want a discussion. "Perfect love. God created a beautiful place for Adam and Eve to live in perfect relationship with Him. They were to accept him as father, and he would keep them in his perfect love. Just as so many fathers do today."

To her consternation and obvious surprise, the sound

of sobbing broke her narrative. Judy had lost her composure and was being consoled by Martha. Harry was deeply moved, but Hamish held his head in his hands. Roger had a comforting arm around him. Jeanne waited until she could resume. "When Adam and Eve broke his single rule – not to eat from the one tree – God had to act. You see, God is the source of perfect justice. God cannot tolerate anything that is not wholly good. He cannot compromise, because he is perfect goodness."

Hamish's voice was quiet but determined. "I think justice is so important. Those who break the law should pay the price and face the consequences."

Jeanne nodded in agreement. "When we hear of, or even see a crime today, we all immediately want justice, don't we? One of the first sayings a young child learns is 'that's not fair' – to which the adult normally replies, 'life isn't fair'. True? Our sense of justice is built in, because it comes from God in creation. But notice this. Our sense of justice is frequently motivated by revenge, or uncontrolled anger, or outrage. Look at God's response to the crime committed by Adam and Eve. Is it outrage? Is it uncontrolled anger? Is it revenge? No!"

Jeanne coughed and went on. "We could say that God had every right to act however he wanted but look again. He acts in love! If you had given a beautiful gift to a child of your own, the best you could afford, and the child smashed it up in temper, how would you respond? Look what God did! He responded proportionately, but his love was not taken from them. Their circumstances were changed, so there was punishment, but it was fair. And the rest of the Bible is the story of how God opened up a way for people to be restored to the fullness of life."

Harry raised a hand. "What do you mean, Jeanne? What do you mean by fullness of life?"

"Life as God wanted it in the beginning for everyone before Adam and Eve broke his rules."

"And how does he restore that today?"

"Through sending his son to die for you." Jeanne looked him in the eye. "In your place."

Harry went pale. "I'm a father myself. There's no way and no circumstances in which I could imagine sending my child to die. But God did that for me?"

Jeanne lowered her voice. "Yes. Like us all, we deserve our punishment because none of us are good. God is perfect and we are all guilty. We cannot come up to his standards. It's impossible. But Jesus took the punishment for you. You and I, all of us here, we should have had the flogging, the spittle, the shame of being hung up naked on a tree in sight of everyone who came by."

Harry began to shake before speaking, the tremor in his voice clearly audible. "I do deserve that."

Jeanne paused. "We are all in the same boat. But Jesus opens the way for us to return to a relationship with God for ever."

"What do I have to do, Jeanne? Where is this way?"

"Believe. Just believe. Tell Jesus you accept you have done wrong. He will bring you in his power through death with him, to life in heaven."

Harry took a deep breath. "Even with what I've done in my life?"

"Yes. He forgives you and comes to live in your heart. And he takes all your guilt and wrongdoing away so it is like a fresh start, but in a relationship that will last, where he will never leave you."

Harry bowed his head. Martha intervened. "Jeanne, I asked you before to explain why God allowed Adam and Eve to do all these bad things in the first place, and why he still lets people do as they want today. Why didn't he just stop them? Can you answer that one for me now?"

Jeanne nodded. "Yes, many people ask that question. Why did God allow this to happen? Why did he put the tree in the garden and place a ban on the consumption of its fruit? You can find the answer in your own ability to love others. That ability comes from God. To understand what God is doing, you need to ask yourself to define the greatest gift you can give a fellow human being. Wealth? No, it just brings a desire for more. Wealth is never enough. Health? No, because death eventually occurs anyway. A great relationship? No, although none of these gifts are intrinsically bad. Relationships can be spoiled by changing circumstances, other people, other ideas. No, the answer is the gift of freedom. Freedom to choose. Free will. God allows people to choose whether they want his love or not. Free will is fundamental to human happiness."

Jack looked thoughtful. "So just one more time, are

we talking a kind of perfection here? Is that what God is? Perfect?"

Jeanne smiled and picked up the thread again. "Perfect in love, perfect in justice. And through the work of Jesus, perfect peace."

Jack looked serious. "So what did Jesus actually do before he died? Where can we find all of that?"

Jeanne looked at him. "If you haven't read Mark's Gospel, you need to do that. It opens with the assertion that Jesus is the Son of God. As you read it, you will find why Mark is certain of that fact. Have a look now, verse one of chapter one. Mark is certain. And Mark is a guy who was there to see it for himself. He is an eyewitness."

She opened her arms dramatically. "If someone makes an extraordinary claim, what do you do? If you are like me, you probably dismiss the claim as rubbish, simply because it is extraordinary. But if you get over that, you then want evidence. Proof. Yes? So what proof does Mark give us? Let me summarise this for you. You can check out what I tell you later in the Bible, at your leisure.

If God created the world, he must have power over it. Over death, sickness, nature, and evil. Everything. I challenge you to read it. It's not too long, but it is fascinating. Mark tells how he saw Jesus bring a little girl back from the dead, and Lazarus back to life three days after he had passed away. Funny phrase, I think, because it is used as a softer way of announcing a death, but if you pass away, you must be going somewhere.

The woman with the haemorrhage – read that one! This was a woman who had what she thought was an incurable disease. She wanted to just touch Jesus. She pushed through the crowd and just for a moment held a part of his cloak. Jesus feels power flowing out from him as she is healed from a condition the doctors had failed to remedy, lots more too. Mental and physical sickness.

And then there's nature. Jesus calms a storm. When you read it, see how the storm stops immediately and the lake becomes calm. The storm we had here last week whipped the Mersey into a very choppy waterway, and when the wind dropped, it was still pretty unsettled for a good while. Jesus commanded it and the storm obeyed. Feeding four or five thousand people with a little food is unnatural, you might say, but Jesus did it in front of a huge number of witnesses. It happened. He commanded nature because He is the Son of God. The evil spirits were forced to obey him too. Read the book later as I suggested. Mark tells you what he saw. Mark was there."

She paused a moment. "Jesus is proven by Mark, and many other witnesses, to be the Son of God."

Jack sat back in his chair. "Jeanne, can you explain more about why Jesus had to come? Couldn't God have sorted it all out in an easier way?"

Jeanne leaned forward in her chair.

"Let me tell you in more detail. We agreed that we all get stuff wrong, didn't we? Mess things up. Do things we know are wrong, but something impels us to do them anyway. Not telling truth, stealing, being dishonest with our taxes, taking advantage of people weaker than ourselves, getting into relationships we shouldn't have and doing what we should not, failing to do what we should. If your life – and mine – was a movie, there's a lot you would be proud for people to see. Great kids, maybe, sporting triumph, musical prowess, academic achievements, and that's all very good. But there would be plenty of scenes you would not want others to see. Websites you are ashamed of visiting, bad things we have done, causing hurt to others and so much more – just think through your own life and feel the weight of that guilt and you'll know it is true of you. It's true for everyone. We can't deal with the guilt, it won't go away, we can't undo what we have done."

"So tell me again, what can we do?" Jack's question was earnest.

"Like I said, we can't do anything other than believe and turn back to God. As you will see as you come to know your Bible better, the story of the Jewish people before Jesus is one of honest effort and complete failure. They tried to live up to God's commands, but they couldn't. So, they made sacrifices from the stuff they owned, animals and birds, and burned them to make up. They went off, tried again, and were back making up for what they had done with more sacrifices. God's plan was to make the perfect sacrifice that would stop all this from happening. Our doing things is futile because it can never be enough. Jesus was that perfect sacrifice when he was killed on the cross."

Simone shifted uneasily in her chair. "That takes my breath away, Jeanne. It's so personal."

Jeanne extended her arms again. "Accept him then. Tell him you are sorry. God will start to turn you back into the person you were created to be." She looked imploringly at her listeners and sat down.

Pete allowed a few moments for her words to sink in before he stood. "Wow, Jeanne, what a message. Thank you. Can we just round things off now? When you started, you mentioned five issues you had picked up from us, and I am sure you have dealt with those in what you have said and in what you have asked us to read. But can you just specifically summarise those five points before we start to bring things to a close for today?"

Jeanne returned to her feet waved her index finger towards him. "I still have one more point to make, Pete, and it's from one Roger made on our first day with you. Forgiveness is perfect in God. But before we pick that one up, yes, let's go back to where we began, to those questions.

Why good people don't go to heaven? They do! But only if they accept what Jesus did for them and respond accordingly. Why do bad things happen to good people? Because evil lives in people's hearts and the effect is random. Evil affects everyone. War, murder, terrorism and other terrible events all begin in one person's heart and from their evil desires. And death? It is the result of the broken creation. Broken by people. Including you and me.

If we say yes, we believe in Jesus and we want our relationship with the perfect father to be put right, we are promised – for certain – that we will have this in eternal life. We will live in heaven after we die on earth, in a new and perfect creation where evil will not exist. Simple. Mark's fellow disciple John was given an amazing insight into what awaits us. It's in the last book of the Bible. That is for another day. But I'm going to ask Yvon to sing that song once more so you can reflect on our discussions, and because the lyrics really carry one final point I have to make."

CHAPTER 21

Jeanne sat down. Yvon sang more quietly and slightly more slowly to allow every word of the song to be heard and their implication taken in. His slight French inflection only made the lyrics more poignant. The mood in the room was of stunned reflection.

The song's lyrics weren't easy. Yvon had sung about how Jesus had opened a way for everyone who wanted to be saved to come to the perfect father, and it included abusers. That was a tough one to take. Murderers. Those responsible for genocide, for people trafficking. For torture. And for everyone in that gathering.

Jack broke the silence. "I can see how I can forgive most things, but not people who ruin the lives of others. Surely they have to go to hell."

Jeanne said nothing. She spent a full minute in contemplation before rising to her feet. "May I invite anyone who needs forgiveness to come and join me at the front?"

Martha was first. Roger followed. Then, one by one,

they came out until no-one remained seated. Judy was last up.

Jeanne acknowledged them all. "Thank you. Tell me, do you want your heavenly father to forgive you for your guilt and your sin, whatever it is, and all you are ashamed of, and give you a new start?"

Jack spoke the thoughts in each heart. "We do." An individual murmur of assent followed from every one of them.

"Then it is all forgiven. And in God's power, we are made able to forgive others in the same way. Let's take a moment to think of the people who have caused us offence and hurt, maybe very seriously, in our lives, whom we have not been able to forgive. Now, forgive each one in turn, bringing a picture of them to your mind and silently tell them their sin is forgiven. Totally forgotten. As if it never happened. Can you do that?"

The serious nature of the moment reflected on each face. Jeanne prayed. "Father, we know your forgiveness comes because your son died to pay the penalty which is rightly ours. He was killed in our place. We thank you for your unconditional love and mercy. We want to accept your gift and promise today to live for you in your power, freedom and peace. Be with us and help us."

Jeanne looked up. "Before we finish, there are two things I need to add. Firstly, I hope you can see where you can find the answers to all the questions you have raised since we came here.

Secondly, can we all see how judgemental we are as

humans? I think each of us has passed judgement on at least one other person in this room in the recent past. Even when we read a story, we find ourselves judging the fictional characters and highlighting their wrongdoing to give ourselves a warm feeling that we are not like them. We grow in our self-righteousness, don't we? And if we don't know for sure, we make it up. Have you suspected someone based on circumstantial evidence? And judged them on that basis? I think we have all done that. But today, God has given us his own perfect righteousness through forgiveness, because we were all in the dock and found guilty, but Jesus has taken the punishment we deserve. He does that for every person who asks, be they murderers, traffickers, or even abusers.

May I suggest that we take a couple of minutes out now for some quiet time, to think through the mighty things we have all just prayed? Let God speak to you in your own heart."

A full two minutes went by before Jeanne brought them back together. "Many of us have the most painful and damaging memories from the past. We all had burdens of guilt to lay down and leave with the Lord. My prayer is that you did just that, and that you will experience his life and resurrection power for yourselves. Were you able to do that?"

Amid the murmur of assent, one voice was raised.

"Yes, from my heart." The voice was Harry's.

"Then Dilys would be so proud of you." Jeanne affirmed quietly.

Judy spoke after a short pause. "Thank you, Jeanne. It is so good to reconnect with the foundation of your faith like this, even when you are a Christian for a long time."

Jeanne smiled and decided it was the moment to tease her friend. "It may even be a very long time, Judy!"

Judy grinned and affected remonstration. "Jeanne, I'm shocked! I have shared confidential concerns with you many times over my appearance, and here you are saying how old I look, in front of other people! I thought you were my friend!"

Jeanne's eyes shone at the banter. "Sorry, Judy. I should have known. How very insensitive of me. I do apologise!"

Judy's eyes matched her friend's. "I forgive you."

Jeanne laughed. Before Roger closed the meeting, he had some information for the group.

"There is some good news," began Roger "about our friend Hamish. You may know that he had to leave us suddenly in the middle of our meeting last week, and we may have been wondering why. He told me that his son had gone missing in Scotland – yes, really – and he has been through the mill emotionally as you will imagine. Hamish came back on Sunday evening and I'm sure he was fearing the worst. Judy and I prayed for him. Tonight, he phoned me to say that the police had called to tell him his son had been found. It's an amazing outcome for Hamish, and maybe an answer to prayer."

Pete stood beside Roger. "There's one other item of news, but I'm going to have to save that. Our visitors are returning to France on Thursday evening. That's the day after tomorrow. Can we give them a nice send off at the airport? I'll ring round everyone with a meeting point and time, plus one other urgent question."

Wednesday's drizzle didn't dampen Pete's enthusiasm. He called Harry and they met Judy and Roger for lunch. Jeanne and Yvon were out in Liverpool, taking in the museums and galleries around the Albert Dock. Pete sat by Judy, leaving Roger and Harry on the other side of the table. Pete took the order and asked Harry to help him with carrying the drinks back from the counter. They got up and joined the queue. This was the John Lewis café and it was busy.

Over lunch, Roger, Judy and Harry discovered a shared knowledge of Surrey and the home counties. The three of them were animatedly recounting tales of derring-do in places from the past. But Pete had a significant question to ask.

"Roger, Judy, do you feel any sense of calling to remain with us as our pastors in the future? Is the Lord asking you to stay in Liverpool? Has anything changed since we last discussed the subject?"

Roger was ready for the question. "Well, we've enjoyed the whole unexpected adventure. Your people here are real, with their own strengths and weaknesses which they see. There is work to be done, for sure, and we agree, you need a trained leader who is both a teacher and a pastor. Judy and I are going to pray for you. God didn't bring us here for an interview and a new job, but for another reason. Therefore, we are returning to Paris, where we have our own challenges to meet. God will find the way forward for you, we know that. You have our thanks and our best wishes."

Harry shook his head sadly and looked at Roger and Judy. "Just when we were starting to get on so well. That's a shame. There's so much more to talk about, you know, from the old days. We might even know some people in common."

Roger nodded. "That's life, Harry. We'll have another chat at the airport before we leave."

CHAPTER 22

"Are you sure we are doing right?" The questioner was Judy. Thursday had arrived and the Eldermen were packing. "The stakes are high, you know. We are talking about people's lives."

Roger seemed determined, hardening his jaw. "Judy, we are going through with the plan. The stakes are high, but they are high in Paris as well as in Liverpool. But I'm going to give Jeanne a call and have a coffee with her. Yvon will be happy with a little extra free time in the city."

The John Lewis café wasn't humming. It was absolutely buzzing. They found a table near the corner. Jeanne leaned across to Roger. "Will she be ok? Isn't all this change going to mess about with her head?"

"I don't know. We have to trust not. I mean, she felt more secure in France because she was away from the scene of what happened, then she was prepared to go back to Surrey and face it but ended up in Liverpool. She asked me if I was sure that us going back was God's will. I told her my hunch was so, and that we were going with the plan."

"What about Pete? What is he going to do? Why are they all coming to see us off? We could have said our farewells on Tuesday."

"I'm not sure what's going on." Roger's expression changed. "They all seem to be nice people, so maybe they see it as an act of kindness to us. Pete was ringing round everyone yesterday, so nothing would surprise me! I'll get Harry to pick us up after he's done that little job for me, so a bit earlier than he'd said, to allow time for whatever Pete has in mind."

Harry arrived punctually at the earlier time requested by Roger and immediately handed over the message in the sealed envelope from the dental surgery. Jeanne sat in the front whilst the other three squeezed into the back. She relieved Yvon of his guitar to alleviate matters. Harry tried to fit it in the boot with four cabin bags and two substantial suitcases, all of which were fuller than on arrival, but to no avail, so it travelled on Jeanne's lap. Roger, Judy and Harry carried on where their previous chat had left off.

Harry parked in the short stay and the party moved to the terminal. Pete had commandeered a seating area and everyone had turned up. Harry carried the rest of the luggage, neatly assembling it in the middle. Roger excused himself, slipped away and quickly glanced at the contents of the envelope with Hamish, who had followed him. The two men swapped glances and

Hamish put the letter in his pocket. They returned several minutes later to find conversations in full flow. It was Pete who motioned everyone to be silent.

"Our gratitude to you knows no limits. Dearest Dilys has had her hand on this throughout not only these days we have spent together, but before then too. We have been trying to discern what we should do with her legacy so that it reflects her wishes for us all. Before she died, Dilys saw our needs, and arranged for us to be brought together in faith and forgiveness through the visit of Jeanne, Yvon, Judy and Roger.

But even Dilys's will is superseded by a greater one, that of God himself. I have spoken to Roger earlier today after ringing you all yesterday, and we both agree that he and Judy must return to Paris and complete what they have begun there." He glanced at Roger who raised a finger.

"Thank you, Pete. We must do that. But I have something to tell you. When we set off from Paris, we were heading for Gatwick and our old stamping ground in Surrey. I had friends standing by with accommodation. It was Jeanne who, without my knowledge, had booked tickets to bring us to Liverpool, because she knew it was what the Lord wanted. And she was right.

For the return flight, I agreed to book the tickets. I have to tell you that I have actually reserved six tickets in total."

Harry grinned playfully. "Pete and I would be delighted to accept! How very kind!"

Roger thought of the envelope and bit his lip. "Harry, we would be pleased to see you there. I really hope that you will be coming over one day, but I'm afraid your name is not on my tickets. Four of them are for our flight today, and two more for a date quite soon. Speaking of flights, Yvon, would you and Judy go to the bag drop and get the cases and the guitar checked in? Jeanne and I will join you airside, when we get through security."

Yvon and Judy acquiesced. Farewells were brief but touching.

Harry had ceased grinning.

CHAPTER 23

Jeanne and Pete were speaking confidentially and quietly. When they had finished, it was Roger's turn to take Pete aside to resume his own narrative. Hamish moved to stand next to him as he did so. "You see, Dilys and Jeanne were friends for a very long time. When Jeanne found out about some problems Judy still suffers because of issues in her childhood, she mentioned them to Dilys, seeking advice. But Dilys had a hunch she could do more. Can I say it was divine inspiration? Maybe. There was a man she had met who, she thought, may have had an involvement in Judy's past. To prove it, Dilys went back to her old workplace and asked if they would co-operate privately in a DNA test, using evidence from toothbrushes.

Jeanne and I worked with her and I picked up Judy's toothbrush. Dilys did her bit and got Harry's. Then we hit a problem. Dilys lost some mobility. But she was not to be defeated. She got Harry to take a parcel to the dentist's surgery. It contained his own toothbrush. This afternoon, Harry collected the results for us. The DNA matched. Dilys's hunch was right. We had the man we were looking for."

Roger took a deep breath. "I don't know what you were thinking when Hamish left our meeting without a word. Dilys had given him a lead to follow, as you may remember him telling us. That lead involved returning to Surbiton. Judy's family are from there, and it was to there that we were going to go. Hamish was following matters up. Do you remember we heard a buzz in that chapel meeting? Hamish left quickly because he had a train to catch. The buzz was his phone alarm.

Hamish here returned soon afterwards. The purpose of his trip had been to verify a story which involved a man by the name of Henry. According to Dilys, this Henry may have repeatedly committed a crime which was sickening and odious. He had never been caught after changing his appearance and falsifying his identity.

Hamish led the new investigation of the whole thing. His enquiry revealed a suspicion that Henry had moved to Merseyside to live under a new name. Back in the day, as you may know, Dilys had always taken her responsibilities seriously. Right at the start of all this, she knew that she had a duty to report her initial concerns to the local police. It was, without being too specific, a child abuse issue."

Pete's expression changed. "Roger, some time ago, there was an abuse investigation which even reached our group. But we were given an all clear. We lost a few members though, no smoke without fire and all that. Was that relevant to what you are saying now?"

"Yes, it was. But the police didn't find the man. They were foxed by the change of name. Then the concern Dilys had came to their attention. They made enquiries around here about her issue. There were no records of any similar problems involving anyone up here, neither from the community nor from the workplace. However, as a result of their work, they felt they were closing in on the truth, and therefore on the perpetrator."

Pete's face fell. "Is it someone we know?"

Roger looked at Hamish for reassurance. His tone was grave. "Yes. We are talking about a very serious matter here as you both know. There are proper procedures to be followed which take time, the police will see to that. But if charges are pressed by the sufferer of his actions, the victim will certainly see that justice is done in the eyes of the law."

The threesome returned solemnly to re-join Harry and Jeanne. A hush fell over the two of them as they saw the faces approaching them. They knew something serious was afoot.

Harry managed a weak smile. "Jeanne, you touched me deeply with what you said. Forgiveness is such a powerful force."

Pete stared at the floor. "There's no easy way to tell you this. God has been leading us forward, but his ways are not always easily understood. What is happening here is uncomfortably close to home. Hamish and Roger have confirmed that our group may be depleted for the foreseeable future."

Harry stood quickly to his feet. "Look after that for me, mate." He gave Roger his car key and one moment later, he was gone.

"Is he ok?" Pete glanced at Hamish. "Shall I go and find him?"

Hamish held up his hand as his mobile buzzed. This time there was no alarm, and there was no need to find Harry. A few minutes later, he was on his way to the local police station after handing himself over to a uniformed officer outside the terminal building.

Hamish whispered confidentially to the others. "We had the exits covered. We had a tail on him since he left to go to pick up the test results."

Jeanne broke into their puzzlement. "I know this may be hard to do, but can we all pray for Harry as well as for Judy?"

Perplexed heads nodded but no-one spoke. Jeanne went ahead. "Father, loving father, give Judy the strength she needs, increase your power at work in her as she looks to the future. We pray for our brother Harry, who needs an extra sense of your presence with him as he faces such uncertainty over his future. We thank you that we can all turn to you in sorrow for our sins, and we entrust our whole group to your care. Amen."

"Amen."

Hamish allowed a moment to pass. His face changed to look of perplexed confidentiality. "I also have something to tell you. I told you something which was untrue. My son didn't go missing. I don't even have a son. It wasn't true, but I had to think of something to explain my absence, and the emotion I showed. I'm not even a Christian. It's very hard for a career detective to see evil dealt with as you have done. I need time to process what has happened, but instead of the usual hatred and bitterness at the end, I seem to be sensing love."

Pete's voice was subdued. "Why did you break down then, when we were discussing God as the heavenly father?"

Hamish looked at him. "I got upset because my wife and I are unable to have children, and the message you were hearing about a perfect father just got to me. That's why I specialised in abuse cases, you know, to do something positive. What I didn't tell you was that I was in the road outside the scout hut because Dilys had planned our meeting there. She told me how she was moving things forward to help me discover the truth. I was sent up here by the Surrey police to work, shall we say undercover, with their local colleagues. The case down there was never closed."

An eerie calm descended as the gravity of the situation returned and the truth about the outcome of what Dilys had initiated sank in. It was fully five minutes before Pete summoned the courage to lift their spirits. "One more thing. When I called everyone yesterday, we were of one mind. We feel that God is calling us to ask you to lead us, but it isn't Roger and dear Judy. Jeanne, we want you and Yvon to come and pastor us. You seem perfect for the job."

Roger smiled. "That's why I booked six tickets. When they have finished their training placement with us in France, they will use the other two to fly back to Liverpool." He looked at the others. "And trust me, I promise not to divert anyone to Gatwick!"

Jeanne's grin was broad. "Wonderful, thank you. I am honoured. Yvon and I will get onto all the paperwork to be done as soon as we get back."

At that moment, the revolving door spun and Jack returned, closely followed by Simone and Martha.

It was Simone who explained. "We were on our way back when we realised we'd forgotten to give you a present each. They were in the boot of Jack's car. I was hoping we would get here before you went through. Where's Judy? Where's Yvon?"

Roger explained. "They've gone ahead. Simone. We're still here because we've had a lot to chat about." He looked at what they were carrying. "I can tell you one thing though – I'm glad you did catch us! Do you know what though? I'm really pleased you three were travelling together. I thought you didn't get on too well."

Jack laughed. "I don't know where you got that idea from."

Martha handed over the bottle of champagne she was carrying. "Simone and Jack came for a coffee in my lounge at home. We all had a good chat and they have decided to forgive each other and set aside their differences. I do hope it works out in practice, as the chapel will be so much nicer if they are not at each other's throat all the time. They both agreed to make a fresh start."

Simone nodded animatedly. "So, when Jack offered Martha and me a lift to see you off, I firstly checked with him that he wouldn't be driving the company car, you know, the one with the big space and the silver rails in the back, to the airport. He said he wouldn't be seen dead in it. So, I agreed. Jack said he would be delighted because it would mean I wouldn't have to go on the bus, so I simply couldn't let him down. So here we are."

Her eyes shone as she looked around the group. "Sorry, I digress." She handed over the bottle in her hand, and Jack passed two more to Jeanne. "I know this is coals to Newcastle, but we've got you a bottle of champagne each to take home. Can you pass one each to the other two, with our love?"

Roger grinned. "We'll definitely squeeze those into the cabin bags!"

Jeanne shook her head as Roger's air of confidence eroded. "We can't. Security won't let us. Jack, can you keep them for when Yvon and I come back? It will be lovely for everyone if we celebrate together then."

Jack nodded before taking his moment. "Shame, Simone bought them for you from a budget supermarket."

Simone smiled. "I can't argue back because he is my lift home!"

Roger was looking suitably disappointed over the gifts. "I would have served mine with the starter on our first dinner back in Paris."

Pete smiled. "We'll toast you and Judy when Yvon and Jeanne return. Jack will drink your share. There should be enough with four bottles!"

Roger froze. "Four bottles. You know what, that's what's in a Jereboam. That is a remarkable coincidence."

Jack had one more thing to say. "Hamish McDonald, whatever you do, it's been good getting to know you. You Scots are a canny breed!"

"We are." Hamish laughed, relieved that the recent tension had melted. "Oh, and my name isn't Hamish McDonald, Jack! It was my codename for the investigation I was working on up here."

Jack grinned. "Your boss must have quite a sense of humour! He certainly fooled us! What's your real name?"

Hamish returned the grin with an added twinkle. "Fergal McSporran."

Jack rolled his eyes. "I'm not having that. That's for your next case!"

Final farewells were made. Security done, Yvon's face lit up as Jeanne took the chance to tell him that they would be returning to lead the chapel. Judy's smile was broad.

Roger nudged Jeanne before addressing Judy and

Yvon. "You two go and get a drink. I just want a quick word with Jeanne."

They did. Roger looked at Jeanne. "What happens now?"

"From Harry's point of view? Well, I actually asked Dilys that question some time ago. Obviously, she didn't know he'd be in custody now, but she thought that God was already involved in Harry's life, despite his doubts, and that God would keep on changing him. From Judy's point of view, she will need to be told the truth when the time is right. Not now. There will be some liaison with Hamish anyway. When God's time is right, it will happen, I know Judy will find the strength to forgive him, bless her, but it will need a lot of work, counselling and patience to do that, and even more to rebuild any sort of relationship after that. But you know what? Through the power of God, Judy will experience full healing."

Jeanne looked Roger in the eye. "And our chapel too. Dilys wanted us to become a community where God would be known, where the good news of salvation and eternal life could be taught, where people from all circumstances would come for forgiveness, and where his love and power could be experienced."

Jeanne checked that Judy was still out of earshot before asking a question. "Would Harry be able to come back, Roger? Could that happen one day?"

"Perhaps, Jeanne, perhaps. Who will it be harder for? But it's not up to us to choose the type of sinner we welcome as Christians. It may well be that Harry has repented. God forgives everyone who does that. Only God knows the state of Harry's heart, but maybe one day, he will come back. Remember Yvon's song? It sounds like he'll have to be singing that again when he and you come back permanently."

They strolled across to sit with Yvon and Judy. It was the latter who spoke first. "Roger, I am glad we are going back. We aren't giving up the mission. Jonah went to Nineveh because God got him there. But he didn't stay either. I'm looking forward to getting back to Paris."

Jeanne motioned to the others to draw close. "There's one more thing I feel I should share with you now, since we are going to lead the chapel. Pete wanted me to tell you. It's about him."

Roger smiled. "He did seem a natural leader, didn't he? I felt Dilys would have been proud of the way he dealt with everything after she passed away. I thought that he seemed like a son to her. It was the way he was so committed to continuing her work which impressed me."

Jeanne smiled again. "Dilys would be proud of him. When I first met her, she had no-one in her life. No friends, no family. She'd been cut off. Do you know why?"

Roger shook his head.

"She had a child as a teenager. In those days, society wasn't as tolerant as it is today. Especially in a Welsh village."

Roger nodded. "What happened?"

"The baby boy was taken from her and put in an orphanage in England. She was widely condemned and sent away."

Jeanne clasped her hands together. "The truth was that she'd been raped by the next-door neighbour. She was traumatised to the extent that she couldn't tell anyone about him. He went to church every Sunday without fail. Who would have believed her?

Some weeks later, she found she was pregnant. In the village, of course, her morals became the main topic of conversation. People immediately leapt to the wrong conclusion about Dilys and ostracised her. Her parents – regular church goers – faced with a future full of shame, sent her away to have the baby in England."

Roger shook his head in disbelief.

Jeanne continued. "I guess that's why she knew so much about forgiveness. She forgave the neighbour, her mum and dad, the gossips in the village, everyone. She then spent her life searching for her baby. She never went back to her parents. That was about the time I got to know her."

Tears welled up in Jeanne's eyes. "It was so sad. Anyway, you may have been trying to work out why Pete has seemed so desperate to keep her work going, and why he wants to ensure the chapel stays on the journey Dilys was leading. You are probably asking why he was named to be in charge of her legacy and trusted to do what she would have wanted. Why was it him?"

Jeanne paused before lowering her voice. "She found her child eventually, Roger. His name was Pete."

Roger gaped. "Why didn't everyone get to know when Dilys knew? I don't understand."

"I think she knew that her true family was the family of God. She just wanted him to be saved. No-one else needed to know, and there was no good reason to rake up the past. In her mind, it was as if nothing had ever happened, because God's forgiveness was like that. The secret was between mother and son. Dilys was a truly remarkable woman."

Judy, Yvon and Jeanne were all on the verge of tears. Roger alone was able to acknowledge her words. "Yes, Jeanne, yes, she was."

Judy composed herself briefly. "She would have been a great mum, wouldn't she, to Pete?"

Jeanne reached out for Judy's hand and squeezed it. "She was. She couldn't have loved him more."

Lightning Source UK Ltd.
Milton Keynes UK
UKHW041103281020
372376UK00002B/281

9 781913 264833